Zane squeezed her hand and, leaning toward her, drew her into his arms.

He hadn't planned to kiss her. But at that moment it seemed the most natural thing in the world.

Her lips parted, her breath warm and sweet. He felt a quiver run through her, his pulse kicking up as his mouth dropped to hers.

Dakota gently pushed him away. "Sorry, but your reputation precedes you."

He heard the slight tremble in her voice. She pulled free of his arms and he leaned back, telling himself he shouldn't have kissed her. Especially given why they were together. Didn't he have enough women problems right now?

"You're going to believe rumors about me?" he joked as he tried to cover up how even that quick kiss had affected him.

She smiled, but there was hurt in her gaze.

His gaze caressed her face for a moment before he met her eyes. "But that kiss? I was just fulfilling a promise I made you before you moved to New Mexico. Remember?"

USA TODAY Bestselling author

B.J. DANIELS

WRANGLED

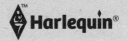

TORONTO NEW YORK LONDON
AMSTERDAM PARIS SYDNEY HAMBURG
STOCKHOLM ATHENS TOKYO MILAN MADRID
PRAGUE WARSAW BUDAPEST AUCKLAND

This book is dedicated to Julie Miller and Delores Fossen, two fellow Intrigue writers I greatly admire. I was with them in Los Angeles relaxing at the *RT Book Reviews* convention when I came up with the ending to this book.
Thank you both for your friendship. I'm looking forward to our January Ice Lake anthology together.

ISBN-13: 978-0-373-69620-8

WRANGLED

Copyright © 2012 by Barbara Heinlein

PLEASE RECYCLE • THIS PRODUCT IS RECYCLABLE

Recycling programs for this product may not exist in your area.

www.Harlequin.com

Printed in U.S.A.

ABOUT THE AUTHOR

USA TODAY bestselling author B.J. Daniels wrote her first book after a career as an award-winning newspaper journalist and author of thirty-seven published short stories. That first book, *Odd Man Out*, received a four-and-a-half-star review from *RT Book Reviews* and went on to be nominated for Best Intrigue that year. Since then, she has won numerous awards, including a career achievement award for romantic suspense and many nominations and awards for best book.

Daniels lives in Montana with her husband, Parker, and two springer spaniels, Spot and Jem. When she isn't writing, she snowboards, camps, boats and plays tennis. Daniels is a member of Mystery Writers of America, Sisters in Crime, International Thriller Writers, Kiss of Death and Romance Writers of America.

To contact her, write to B.J. Daniels, P.O. Box 1173, Malta, MT 59538 or email her at bjdaniels@mtintouch.net. Check out her website, www.bjdaniels.com.

Books by B.J. Daniels

HARLEQUIN INTRIGUE

*Whitehorse, Montana
‡‡Whitehorse, Montana: The Corbetts
**Whitehorse, Montana: Winchester Ranch
‡Whitehorse, Montana: Winchester Ranch Reloaded
†Whitehorse, Montana: Chisholm Cattle Company

CAST OF CHARACTERS

Zane Chisholm—The moment the good-looking cowboy saw the strange woman standing on his doorstep, he should have known she was trouble.

Dakota Lansing—The cowgirl came back to Montana for her father's funeral, only to get the shock of her life.

Sheriff McCall Winchester Crawford—She wanted this baby more than anything. But would it mean giving up her job?

Courtney Baxter—Her greatest desire was to get to know her birth mother. But would it mean betraying her sister?

Emma and Hoyt Chisholm—The patriarch and matriarch of Chisholm Cattle Company wanted simply to enjoy their six sons and live happily ever after. Unfortunately, someone had another plan for them.

Mrs. Crowley—The irascible housekeeper made it impossible for anyone to get close to her.

Aggie Wells—She was determined to save Emma from the killer. But could she save herself?

Laura Chisholm—Dead or alive, she was playing havoc with the Chisholm family.

Arlene Evans Monroe—Was she up to her old tricks? Or was she as much in the dark as everyone else?

The Whitehorse Sewing Circle—Another one of the illegal adoptions done by the women was about to come to light.

Chapter One

The knock at the door surprised Zane Chisholm. He'd just spent the warm summer day in the saddle rounding up cattle. All he wanted to do was kick off his boots and hit the hay early. The last thing he wanted was company.

But whoever was knocking didn't sound as if they were planning to go away anytime soon. Living at the end of a dirt road, he didn't get uninvited company— other than one of his five brothers. *So that narrows it down,* he thought as he went to the window and peered out through the curtains.

The car parked outside was a compact, lime-green with Montana State University plates. Definitely not one of his brothers, he thought with a grin. Chisholm men wouldn't be caught dead driving such a "girlie" car. Especially a lime-green one.

Even more odd was the young, willowy blonde pounding on his door. She must be lost and needing directions. Or she was selling something.

His curiosity piqued, he went to answer her persistent knock. As the door swung open, he saw that her eyes were blue and set wide in a classically gorgeous face. She wore a slinky red dress that fell over her body like water. The woman was a stunner.

She smiled warmly. "Hi."

"Hi." He waited, wondering what she wanted, and enjoying the view in the meantime.

Her smile slipped a little as she took in his worn jeans, his even more worn cowboy boots and the dirty Western shirt with a torn sleeve and a missing button.

"I wasn't expecting company," he said when he saw her apparent disappointment in his attire.

"Oh?" She looked confused now. "Did I get the night wrong? You're Zane Chisholm and this is Friday, right?"

"Right." He frowned. "Did we have a date or something?" He knew he'd never seen this woman before. No red-blooded American male would forget a woman like this.

She reached into her sparkly shoulder bag and pulled out a folded sheet of paper. "Your last email," she said, handing it to him.

He took the paper, unfolded it and saw his email address. It appeared he had been corresponding with this woman for the past two days.

"If you forgot—"

"No," he said quickly. "Please, come in and let's see if we can sort this out."

She stepped in but looked tentative, as if not so sure about him.

"Why don't you start with how we met," he said as he offered her a seat.

She sat on the edge of the couch. "The Evans rural internet dating service."

"Arlene's matchmaking business?" he asked in surprise. Arlene Evans, who was now Arlene Monroe, had started the business a few years ago to bring rural couples together.

"We've been visiting by email until you…"

"Asked you out," he finished for her.

"Are you saying someone else has been using your email?"

"It sure looks that way, since I never signed up with Arlene's matchmaking service. But," he added quickly when he saw how upset she was, "I wouldn't be surprised if Arlene is behind this. It wouldn't be the first time she took it upon herself to play matchmaker." Either that or his brothers were behind it as a joke, though that seemed unlikely. This beautiful woman was no joke.

She looked down at her hands in her lap. "I'm so embarrassed." She quickly rose to her feet. "I should go."

"No, wait," he said, unable to shake the feeling that maybe this had been fate and that he would be making the biggest mistake of his life if he let this woman walk out now.

"You know, it wouldn't take me long to jump in the shower and change if you're still up for a date," he said with a grin.

She hesitated. "Really? I mean, you don't have to—"

"I *want* to. But you have the advantage over me. I don't know your name."

She smiled shyly. "Courtney Baxter." She held out her hand. As he shook it, Zane thought, *This night could change my life.*

He had no idea how true that was going to be.

Chapter Two

Dakota Lansing got the call at 3:20 a.m. She jerked awake, surprised by the sound of the ringing phone. She hadn't had a landline in years. Glancing around in confusion, for a moment she forgot where she was.

Home at the ranch. It all came back in a rush, including her father's death. She turned on the light as the phone rang yet again and grabbed the receiver.

As she did, she glanced at the clock, her mind spinning with fear. Calls in the wee hours of the morning were always bad news.

"Hello?" Her voice broke as she remembered the last call that had come too early in the morning.

This is Dr. Sheridan at Memorial Hospital in Great Falls. I'm sorry to inform you that your father has had a heart attack. I'm afraid there was nothing we could do. Your sister is here if you would like to speak with her.

My sister? You must have the wrong number, I don't have a sister.

"Hello?" she said again now.

At first all she heard was crying. *"Hello?"*

"Dakota, I need your help."

Her sister, half sister, the one she hadn't known existed until two weeks ago, let out a choked sob.

"Courtney? What's wrong?"

More sobbing. "I'm in trouble."

This, at least, didn't come as a surprise. Dakota had expected her half sister was in trouble when she'd asked after their father's funeral if she could stay at the ranch for a while.

"I want to get to know you," Courtney had said. But it had become obvious fairly quickly that her half sister wanted a lot more than that.

"Speak up. I can barely hear you," Dakota said now.

"I can't. He's in the next room."

Dakota rolled her eyes. A man. Not surprising, since Courtney had been out every night in the two weeks since their father's funeral.

"I think he might be dead."

Dakota came wide awake. *Dead?* "Where are you?" There was a loud crash in the background as something fell and broke. "Tell me where you are," Dakota cried as she stumbled out of bed. *"Courtney?"*

Her father's secret love child, a woman only two years younger than herself, whispered two words before the line went dead.

"Zane Chisholm's."

ZANE WOKE TO POUNDING. He tried to sit up. His head swam. He hadn't really drunk champagne last night, had he?

Numbly he realized the pounding wasn't just in his head. Someone was at the door and it was still dark outside. He turned on a light, blinded for a moment. As he glanced over at the other side of his queen-size bed, he was a little surprised to find it empty. Courtney had come home with him last night, hadn't she?

As he got up he saw that he was stark naked. Whoever was at the door was pounding harder now. He quickly pulled on a pair of obviously hastily discarded jeans and padded barefoot into the living room to answer the door.

"What the hell happened to *you?*" his brother Marshall asked in surprise when Zane opened the door.

"I'm a little hungover." A major understatement. He couldn't remember feeling this badly—even during his college days when he'd done his share of partying.

"Your face," Marshall said. "It's all scratched up."

Zane frowned and went into the bathroom. He turned on the light and stared in shock into the mirror. His pulse jumped. He had what looked like claw marks down the side of his left cheek. As he looked down at his arm, he saw another scratch on his forearm.

What the hell had happened last night?

"Are you okay?" Marshall asked from the bathroom doorway. He sounded worried, but nothing like Zane felt.

"I don't know. I'm having trouble remembering last night."

"Well, it must have been a wild one," Marshall said. "I hope it was consensual with whatever mountain lion you hooked up with."

"Not funny." His head throbbed and his memory was a black hole that he was a little afraid to look into too deeply.

"You do remember that you and I are picking up horses in Wolf Point today, right?" Marshall said. "I'll give you a few minutes to get cleaned up, but don't even think about trying to get out of this. I need your help and we're already running late. I told you to be ready at four forty-five."

Zane nodded, although it hurt his head. What time was it, anyway? The clock on the wall read 5:10 a.m. "Could you make me some coffee while I get ready?"

His brother sighed. "Aren't you getting a little too old for partying like this?" he grumbled on his way to the kitchen.

Zane stepped into the bathroom, closed the door and stared into the mirror again. He looked like hell. Worse, he couldn't remember drinking more than a glass or two of champagne, certainly not enough to cause this kind of damage.

He thought about Courtney. She had to have done this to him. He touched his check. What scared him was, what had *he* done to get that kind of reaction from her?

EMMA CHISHOLM HAD been an early riser all her life. She liked getting up before the rest of the world when everything was still and dark. Since marrying Hoyt Chisholm a year ago, she especially liked seeing the sun come up here on the ranch.

As she stepped into the big ranch kitchen, she heard a sound and froze.

"I hope I didn't scare you."

Emma shuddered as a chill raced down the length of her spine. She tried to hide it but knew she'd failed when she turned to see amusement in their new live-in housekeeper's one good eye. Up before sunrise and often the last one to bed, the woman moved around the house with ghostlike stealth.

"There really is no need for you to work such long

hours," she said as Mrs. Crowley stepped out of the dark shadows of the kitchen. The fifty-eight-year-old woman moved with a strange gait—no doubt caused by her disfiguring injury. It was hard to look into Mrs. Crowley's face. The right side appeared to have been horribly burned, that eye white and sightless. Behind her thick glasses, her other eye shone darkly.

"I'm not interested in sleeping anymore," Mrs. Crowley said. Her first name was Cynthia, but she'd asked them to refer to her by her married name.

The moment she'd come to the house, she had taken over. But Emma couldn't complain. Mrs. Crowley, a woman about her own age, was a hard worker and asked for little in return. She lived in a separate wing of the house and was Emma's new babysitter.

Not that Emma's husband, Hoyt, would ever admit that was the case. But last year his past had come back to haunt them. It had to do with the deaths of Hoyt's last three wives. An insurance investigator by the name of Aggie Wells had been convinced that he'd killed them.

When Aggie had heard about Hoyt's fourth marriage—this one a Vegas elopement to Emma—she'd come to Montana to warn Emma that she was next.

Aggie was dead now. While the police hadn't found her killer, Emma was fairly certain that the perpetrator was the same one who'd murdered at least one of Hoyt's wives.

Aggie Wells had originally been convinced that the killer was Hoyt, but as time went on she'd thought Hoyt's first wife might still be alive. Laura had allegedly drowned in Fort Peck Reservoir more than thirty years before. Aggie had even found a woman named Sharon Jones, whom she believed was Laura. Unfortunately, Sharon Jones had disappeared before the police could question her.

For months now Hoyt had been afraid to leave Emma alone. Either he or one of his six sons hung around the house to make sure no harm came to her.

She'd been going crazy, feeling as if she was under house arrest. Hoyt and his sons had to be going crazy as well. They were ranchers and much more at home on the back of a horse than hanging around the kitchen with her.

Finally Hoyt had come up with the idea of a live-in housekeeper. Emma was sure that Mrs. Crowley wasn't what he'd had in mind. But after all the rumors and suspicions that were flying around, it was next to impossible to get anyone to work at the ranch.

Fortunately, Mrs. Crowley had been glad to come. She said she liked that Chisholm Cattle Company was so isolated.

"People stare," she'd said simply when Emma had asked her if she thought she could be happy living this far away from civilization.

She was an abrupt woman who had little to say. Emma knew she should be thankful, but sometimes it would be nice to have someone who would just sit and visit with her. That definitely wasn't Mrs. Crowley, but Emma kept trying.

"I see you've made coffee," Emma said now. "May I pour you a cup? We could sit at the table for a few minutes before Hoyt comes down."

"No, thank you. I'm cleaning the guest rooms today."

Emma could have argued that the guest rooms could wait. Actually, they probably didn't need cleaning. It had been a while since they'd had a guest. But Mrs.

Crowley didn't give her a chance. The woman was already off down the hallway to that wing of the house.

As Emma watched her go, she noticed how the woman dragged her right leg. That's what gave her that peculiar gait, she thought distractedly. Then she heard Hoyt coming downstairs and poured them both a cup of coffee.

It wasn't until she took the mugs over to the table that she realized Mrs. Crowley always made herself scarce when Hoyt was around. Maybe she just wanted to give them privacy, Emma told herself. "Strange woman," she said under her breath.

A moment later Hoyt came into the kitchen, checked to make sure they were alone and put his arms around her. "Good morning. Want to sneak out to the barn with me, Mrs. Chisholm? Zane and Marshall have gone to Wolf Point. Dawson, Tanner and Logan are all mending fences and Colton has gone into town for feed."

She laughed, leaning into his hug. It had been a while since they'd made love in the hayloft.

CYNTHIA CROWLEY WATCHED Emma and Hoyt from one of the guest room windows. They had their arms around each other's waists. Emma had her face turned up to Hoyt, idolization in her eyes. She was laughing at something he'd said.

Cynthia could only imagine.

She let the curtain fall back into place as Hoyt pushed open the barn door and they disappeared inside. As she turned to look around the guest room, she mumbled a curse under her breath. The decor was Western, from the oak bed frame to the cowboy-print comforter. *Emma's doing,* the housekeeper thought as she moved to look at an old photograph on the wall.

It was of the original house before Hoyt had added onto it. The first Chisholm main house was a two-story shotgun. It was barely recognizable as the house in which Cynthia now stood. Hoyt had done well for himself, buying up more land as his cattle business had improved.

On another wall was a photograph of his six adopted sons, three towheaded with bright blue eyes, three dark-eyed with straight black hair and Native American features. In the photo, all six sat along the top rail of the corral. The triplets must have been about eight when the picture was taken, which made the other three from seven to ten or so.

They looked all boy. There was a shadow on the ground in the bottom part of the photograph. Hoyt must have been the photographer, since she was sure the shadow was his.

Now the boys were all raised—not that Emma didn't get them back here every evening she could. All but Zane were engaged or getting married so the house was also full of their fiancées. Emma apparently loved it and always insisted on helping with the cooking.

Not that Cynthia Crowley minded the help—or the time spent with the new Mrs. Hoyt Chisholm. Emma fascinated her in the most macabre of ways.

The new Mrs. Chisholm had definitely been a surprise. A man as powerful and wealthy as Hoyt Chisholm could have had a trophy wife. Instead he'd chosen a plump fifty-something redhead.

"There is no accounting for tastes," the housekeeper said to the empty room as she went to work dusting. Before she'd been hired on, she'd been told about Hoyt's other three wives—and their fates.

"Do you think he killed them?" she'd asked the director of the employment agency where she'd gone to get the job.

"Oh, good heavens, no," the woman had cried, then dropped her voice. "I certainly wouldn't send a housekeeper up there if I thought for a moment..."

Cynthia had smiled. "I'm not afraid of Hoyt Chisholm. Or his wife. I'm sorry, what did you say her name was?"

"Emma. And I've heard she is delightful."

"Yes, delightful," Cynthia grumbled to herself now. At the sound of laughter, she went to the window. Through the sheer curtains she saw Emma and Hoyt coming out of the barn. They were both smiling—and holding hands.

Cynthia Crowley made a rude noise under her breath. "The two of them act like teenagers."

A loud snap filled the air, startling her. It wasn't until she felt the pain that she looked down. She hadn't been aware that she'd been holding anything in her hands until she saw the broken bud vase, and the blood oozing from her hand from where she'd broken the vase's fragile, slim neck.

ONCE THEY HAD THE HORSES loaded at a ranch north of Wolf Point, Marshall suggested they grab lunch. Zane wasn't hungry, wasn't sure he ever would be again. He was anxious to call Courtney and find out what had happened last night.

Stepping outside the café to call her, he realized that he didn't have her number. Nor was she listed under

Courtney Baxter. He tried the couple of Baxters in the Whitehorse area, but neither knew a Courtney.

With no choice left, he called Arlene Evans Monroe at the woman's rural internet dating service that had allegedly put them together in the first place.

"Did you set me up with a woman named Courtney Baxter?" he asked Arlene, trying not to sound accusing. Arlene used to be known as the county gossip. In the old days he wouldn't have put anything past her. But he'd heard she'd changed since meeting her husband Hank Monroe.

"Yes," she said, sounding wary. "Is there a problem?"

"Only that Courtney showed up at my door last night saying I had a date with her through your agency and I didn't have a clue who she was."

"Are you telling me you didn't make a date with this woman?"

"I never even signed up for your dating service. I thought maybe someone had done it as a joke."

"Zane, I have your check right here."

How was that possible? He knew he was still feeling the effects of the hangover; his aching head was finding it hard to understand any of this. But all morning he'd been worried about what had happened last night. He had a very bad feeling and needed to talk to Courtney.

"When does it show that I signed up?" he asked Arlene.

"Two weeks ago."

Two weeks ago? A thought struck him. About two weeks ago he'd come home to find someone had been in his house. Like most people who lived in and around Whitehorse he never locked his doors, so the intruder hadn't had to break in. Nor had the person taken anything that he could see—not even his laptop computer. But enough things had been moved that he'd known someone had been there.

He swore now, realizing that must have been when the person had gone online and signed him up for the dating service—and taken at least one of his checks. He hadn't even noticed any were missing.

"What is the number on that check?" he asked Arlene. She read it off and he wrote it down, seeing that it was a much higher number than the checks now in his checkbook. He wouldn't have missed it for months.

Who went around signing someone up for a dating service? This made no sense. It had to have been one of his brothers. Or his stepmother, Emma? She had made it clear she thought it was time her six rowdy stepsons settled down. Maybe she was behind this.

But neither Emma nor his brothers would have come to his house when he wasn't home, gotten on his computer and then taken one of his checks to pay for the rural dating service. Who then? And why? This was getting stranger by the moment.

"I need Courtney Baxter's telephone number," he told Arlene.

"According to the service policy you agreed to—"

"I didn't agree because I never signed up," he said, trying not to lose his temper. He caught his reflection in the café window and saw the four scratches down his cheek where someone had definitely clawed him.

"Zane, what if I call her and make sure it's all right first? Do you want to hold?"

He groaned, but agreed to wait.

She came back on the line moments later. "She's not

answering her cell phone. I left her a message to call me immediately. I'm sorry, Zane, but that's the best I can do. It's policy."

He swore under his breath. The old Arlene would have handed it over. She would also have asked why he was so anxious to talk to his "date" and the news would have gone on the Whitehorse grapevine two seconds later.

"The moment you hear from her…"

"I'll let you know," she said.

Zane didn't hear anything from Arlene on the long drive back to Whitehorse. He hoped that once he got home there might be a note or something from Courtney.

Not wanting to drag the loaded horse trailer down the narrow lane to the house, Marshall dropped him off by the mailbox on the county road.

"You sure you're going to be all right?" Marshall asked.

He'd been sick all day and still had a killer headache.

"You really did tie one on last night," his brother said, looking concerned. "What were you drinking anyway?"

"I remember having some champagne."

Marshall shook his head. "That all?"

Zane couldn't recall if it had been his idea, but he doubted it. Courtney must have suggested it. "And I only had a couple of glasses, I'm sure."

His brother lifted a brow. "You sure about that?"

He wasn't sure of anything. "Don't worry about me. I'm fine," he lied as he climbed out of the Chisholm Cattle Company truck and headed down the narrow dirt road to his house.

The early summer sun was still up on the western horizon. It warmed his back as he walked. Grass grew bright green around him, the air rich with the sweet scents of new growth. Grasshoppers buzzed and butterflies flitted past. In the distance he could see that there was still snow on the tops of the Little Rocky Mountains.

As he came over a rise, he slowed. A pickup he didn't recognize was parked in front of his house. Courtney? Or maybe one of her older brothers here to kick his butt. He quickened his step, anxious to find out exactly what had happened last night—one way or the other.

Zane was still a good distance from the truck when he saw the woman and realized that it wasn't Courtney. This woman was dressed in jeans, boots and a yellow-checked Western shirt. Her chestnut hair was pulled back into a ponytail. She stood leaning against the truck as if she'd been waiting awhile and wasn't happy about it.

When she spotted him, she pushed off the side of the pickup and headed toward him. As she came closer, his gaze settled on her face. He felt the air rush out of him. She was beautiful, but that was only part of what had taken his breath away.

He'd seen Dakota Lansing only once since she was a kid hanging around the rodeo grounds. She'd been cute as a bug's ear back then and it had been no secret that she'd had a crush on him. But, five years his junior, she'd been too young and innocent so he'd kept her at arm's length, treating her like the kid she was.

The last time he'd seen her he'd happened to run into her at the spring rodeo in Whitehorse. He'd been so surprised to see her—let alone that she'd turned into this beautiful woman—he'd been tongue-tied. She must have thought him a complete fool.

The whole meeting had been embarrassing, but since she'd moved to New Mexico, he'd thought he would never see her again. And yet here she was standing in his yard.

"Dakota?" he said, surprised at how pleased he was to see her.

Smiling, he started toward her, but slowed as he caught her body language. Hands on hips, big brown eyes narrowed, an angry tilt to her head. His brain had been working at a snail's pace all day. It finally kicked into gear to question what Dakota Lansing was doing here—let alone why she appeared to be upset.

She closed the distance between them. "Where is my sister?" Those big brown eyes widened, and he knew she'd seen the scratches on his face just seconds before she balled up her fist and slugged him.

The punch had some power behind it, but it still had less effect on him than her words.

"Your sister?" he asked, taking a step back as he rubbed his jaw and frowned at her. He'd known Dakota Lansing all his life. She didn't have a sister.

Chapter Three

"Courtney Baxter," Dakota said. "The woman I know you were out with last night." She looked as if she wanted to hit him again. Her eyes narrowed. "What did you do to her?"

He rubbed his jaw, feeling as if he was mentally two steps behind and had been since Courtney Baxter had knocked on his door not twenty-four hours before. "Courtney Baxter is your sister?"

"My *half* sister. Where is she?"

His head ached and now so did his jaw. Dakota had a pretty good right hook. "How do you know I was with her?"

"She called me sounding terrified. What did you do to her?"

Taking a step back, he raised both hands. "Hold on a minute. We can figure this out."

"What is there to figure out?" she demanded.

He noticed something he hadn't earlier. Dakota's left hand. No wedding ring. No ring at all. The last time he'd seen her, she'd had a nice-size rock on her ring finger. He'd heard she was engaged to some investment manager down in New Mexico.

She saw him staring at her left hand and stuck her

hands into the back pockets of her jeans, her look daring him to say anything about it.

No chance of that.

"We should put something on those knuckles," he said, having noticed before that her right hand was swelling. Hitting him had hurt her more than it had him. Well, physically at least.

Dakota Lansing. He still couldn't believe that the freckle-faced tomboy who used to stick her tongue out at him had grown into this amazing-looking woman.

"Why don't you come into the house for a minute," he said, and started for the front porch

"Zane, I'm only interested in finding my sister."

"So am I." He left the door open, went into the kitchen and opened the freezer door. By the time he heard her come in he had a tray of ice cubes dumped into a clean dishcloth.

"What did you do to her?" Dakota demanded again from the kitchen doorway.

He motioned to a chair at the kitchen table. "Dakota, you know me. You know I wouldn't hurt anyone."

She didn't look convinced, but she did sit down. He reached for her injured hand, but she quickly took the ice from him, pushing his hand away.

"Courtney said on the phone last night that she was in trouble. I heard something crash in the background. Just before the connection went dead she said your name."

The whole time she'd been talking she was glaring at him, challenging him to come up with an explanation. He wished he could.

"Dakota, I have to be honest with you. I can't remember anything about last night. I woke up this morning alone with these scratches on my face and—" he pushed up his sleeve "—my arm."

Her eyes widened a little when she saw the scratches on his arm. He saw fear flicker in her expression, fear and anger. "How long have you been dating my sister?"

She sounded almost jealous. Which he thought just showed how hungover he was. "I had never laid eyes on her until she showed up at my door last night claiming we had a date," he said. He saw she was having trouble believing it. "I swear it. And I certainly didn't know she was your sister. So how is it I never knew you had a sister?"

"She's my father's love child." Dakota sighed and shifted the ice pack on her swollen knuckles. "I only found out two weeks ago after my father died."

He remembered seeing in the newspaper that her father had passed away. He'd thought about sending a card, but it had been so many years, he doubted Dakota would remember him.

"Are you sure she's even—"

"I saw her birth certificate. It had my father's signature and his name on it. Apparently Courtney's mother and my father got together either when my mother was dying or right after."

He could see how painful this was for her. Dakota had idolized her father, and to find out on his death that he'd been keeping a lover and a sister from her for years…

"So you're claiming that Courtney just showed up at your door?" Dakota asked, clearly not wanting to talk about her father.

Zane told her about his call to Arlene at the dating service, the check someone had used to enroll him and that he was waiting to hear from Courtney, since he, too, was worried about what might have happened last night.

She studied him for a long moment. "So a woman you have never seen before shows up at your door claiming you have a date, and you just go out with her anyway?"

He guessed Dakota had probably heard about his reputation with women. "I didn't want to hurt her feelings."

Her chuckle had a distinct edge to it, and he remembered why he'd always liked her. Dakota had always been smart and sassy. She'd been a daredevil as a kid, always up for just about anything, from climbing the three-story structure that held the rodeo announcer's booth at the fairgrounds, to trying to ride any animal that would hold still long enough for her to hop on. Since her father had raised rodeo stock, she'd had a lot of animals to choose from. He'd liked her a lot. Still did, he thought.

"How well do you know her?" Zane asked.

"Not as well as you know her, apparently," Dakota said, and shoved the ice pack away as she reached for her phone.

"Who are you calling?" He hated to think.

"I'm trying Courtney's cell." She punched in the number and hit Send. "I've been trying to call her all day and—"

At the distant sound of a phone ringing they both froze for an instant. Then, getting to their feet, they followed the muffled ringing.

Zane hadn't gone far when he realized the sound was

coming from his bedroom. He pushed open the door and stepped in, Dakota on his heels.

The ringing seemed to be coming from the bed, but when he drew back the crumpled covers, it was empty. As the phone stopped ringing, no doubt going to voice mail, he knelt down and looked under the bed.

He could just make out the phone in the shadowy darkness under the bed—and what was left of the lamp that had been on the nightstand on the other side of the bed. The lamp lay shattered between the bed and the closet.

Refusing to think about that right now, he reached for Courtney's phone.

It wasn't until he pulled it out and heard Dakota gasp that he noticed the cell phone was smeared with something dark red. Blood.

He dropped the phone on the bed, realizing belatedly that he should never have touched it. He had a bad feeling it would be evidence—against him.

As he turned, Dakota took a step back from him. The frightened look in her eyes hit him like a blow. There were tears in her eyes; the look on her face was breaking his heart.

"I didn't harm your sister. Dakota, you *know* me."

"I *knew* you, Zane, but that was a long time ago."

"Not so long. I haven't changed. Drunk or sober, I would never hurt a woman. You have to believe me." But how could he keep telling himself that nothing bad had happened last night when the evidence just kept stacking up?

They both turned toward the front of the house as they heard a vehicle pull up. Zane moved quickly to look out, hoping it would be Courtney and he could get this cleared up and relieve his mind.

But it wasn't Courtney's lime-green compact with the MSU plates.

It was a Whitehorse County Sheriff's Department patrol SUV.

"Mrs. Crowley," Emma cried when she saw the woman's bandaged hand.

"It's nothing."

"Oh, here, let me see it." She reached for the woman's hand.

"I said it was nothing," Mrs. Crowley said, taking a step back and drawing her hand behind her. Her face had closed up, her one good eye glinting as hard as the tone of her voice.

Emma fell silent. She'd held out hope that she would like the woman Hoyt had hired as her housekeeper-babysitter. Being close in age, she'd thought they might have things in common.

But every time she had reached out to Mrs. Crowley, offering her friendship, it had been quickly rebuffed.

"Just let me do my work," the woman said now. Her wrecked face caught the light; the burn scars looked angrier today than usual.

Unlike Hoyt, Emma made a point of looking Mrs. Crowley in the eye. She refused to be put off by her injuries—or her manner.

Hoyt just steered clear of the woman and often apologized for hiring her.

"She's fine," Emma always said in Mrs. Crowley's defense. She suspected that the woman had trouble getting other positions and couldn't afford to lose this job.

Hoyt paid her well and the living accommodations were probably nicer than any she'd had before. Not that Emma's kindness or the house or the pay had softened Mrs. Crowley in the least.

"Whatever happened to her has made her push people away," Emma told her husband. "We just need to keep trying to make her feel at home here."

Hoyt had been skeptical. "You probably pick up stray dogs, too, don't you? Honey, this time I don't think even you can make that woman civil—let alone happy."

Emma couldn't help but wonder what had happened to Mrs. Crowley that made her like this. She suspected it was more than whatever accident she'd had that had left her disfigured. But Emma doubted she would ever know. It wasn't like Mrs. Crowley was going to tell her anytime soon.

"DID YOU CALL THE SHERIFF?" Zane asked without looking at her as Dakota joined him at the window.

"No." With a sinking feeling, Dakota watched Sheriff McCall Crawford climb awkwardly out of the patrol vehicle. Dakota saw that the sheriff was pregnant, a good seven or eight months along.

"Maybe Courtney called her, or—"

Or Courtney had been found. Dakota didn't let him finish that thought. "Courtney wouldn't have called the sheriff." If her sister had had any intention of calling the sheriff, wouldn't Courtney have done so last night instead of calling her?

Whatever Courtney was up to, Dakota suspected the sheriff was the last person she wanted involved.

"Well, if you didn't call her, and Courtney didn't…" Zane let the thought hang between them.

Dakota glanced over at him, saw his freshly scratched face in the glow of the afternoon sun coming through the window and could guess what was about to happen.

Once the sheriff saw the scratches, she wouldn't need to hear about the phone conversation Dakota'd had with Courtney in the wee hours this morning. Nor would the sheriff need to see the bloody phone from under Zane's bed before hauling him off to jail.

Common sense told Dakota, given the evidence, jail was probably the best place for him. But not if she had any hope of him helping her find her sister.

"Here's what I want you to do," she said as the sheriff's footfalls echoed on the old wooden porch. "Go in the bathroom and stay there. Let me handle this."

Zane shook his head as the sheriff knocked at the front door. "If you think I'm going to hide behind your skirts—"

"What you're *going* to do is help me find Courtney, and you can't very well do that behind bars," Dakota said through gritted teeth as the sheriff knocked again. "Turn on the shower. There's something I haven't told you about Courtney. Now trust me."

She shot him an impatient look and waited until he disappeared into the bathroom and shut the door before she went to answer the sheriff's third knock.

AS THE DOOR SWUNG OPEN, Sheriff McCall Crawford couldn't help her surprise.

"Dakota Lansing?" McCall said. "Haven't seen you in a while." She'd been several years ahead of Dakota and they'd gone to different schools—McCall in Whitehorse, while Dakota had gone to Chinook—but they'd crossed paths because of sports.

"I've been living in New Mexico. I only recently returned. For my father's funeral," she added.

"Yes, I heard. I'm sorry." The sheriff looked past her. "Is Zane around, by any chance?"

"He's in the shower, but you're welcome to come in." She stepped back and McCall entered the house. "He's getting ready so we can go out for dinner."

McCall glanced around the small house. There wasn't much to see. Zane Chisholm obviously wasn't into decorating. She doubted he spent much time here.

"I came out to talk to Zane, but since you're here…" McCall said. "Is there a problem I should know about?"

Dakota looked confused by the question. "A problem?"

"I got a call that there was a domestic disturbance out here."

"When was that?"

"Twenty minutes ago," McCall said.

Dakota let out a laugh. "You didn't really take that call seriously, did you? The closest neighbor is a half mile away. Hard to really see or hear a domestic disturbance, unless of course they said there was gunfire involved."

"True," McCall said. "Unless, of course, *you* made the call."

"I can assure you, I didn't call. But I suspect caller ID would have confirmed that," Dakota said.

The sheriff smiled. She remembered Dakota Lansing as being smart and capable. "Just had to check. Actually the call came from a woman who said she was your sister."

"Courtney?"

McCall saw that she now had Dakota's attention. "Is Courtney Baxter your sister?"

"My half sister. Long story. Why would she make a call like that? I haven't seen her for several days."

"Good question." McCall glanced toward the bathroom door. She could hear the shower still running. Zane Chisholm took an awfully long shower.

As she felt the baby kick, McCall rested her hand on her swollen belly. For a moment she was lost in that amazing feeling. The whole pregnancy had been like this, stolen moments from her job when she felt as if she wanted to pinch herself. She just couldn't believe she and Luke were having a baby.

"Is it possible your sister is jealous?" McCall asked as she turned to leave. "I heard Zane was out with a pretty blonde last night. Apparently they were celebrating rather hard."

Compliments of the Whitehorse grapevine first thing this morning. McCall even knew that Courtney Baxter had been wearing a very sexy red dress. Who needed Twitter? *No one in this county,* she thought.

That Courtney was Dakota Lansing's half sister had come as a surprise. The scuttlebutt now around town was that the girl was the product of an affair Clay Lansing had years ago.

"I actually set up the date," Dakota said. "I knew the two of them would hit it off. Zane and I are just friends. But I can understand why Courtney might be jealous after a date with Zane. He is a catch."

McCall nodded as she glanced into the kitchen and bedroom, saw the unmade bed and figured this was merely a case of sibling rivalry. "Well, you two have a nice supper. Have Zane give me a call when he gets a chance."

As she started for the front door, she heard a cell phone ring from somewhere in the bedroom. "If that's your sister calling, please tell her I'd like to talk to her, too," McCall said, and let herself out.

DAKOTA LET OUT THE BREATH she'd been holding since the moment she'd realized it was Courtney's cell phone ringing. Zane had left it lying on the crumpled covers of the bed. Fortunately it had been out of the sheriff's sight.

She hurried into the bedroom and gingerly picked up the phone. Private caller. "Hello?"

No answer, but she could hear breathing on the line. "Who is this? Courtney? If that's you—"

Whoever it was hung up.

Dakota stood holding the phone for a moment, then quickly dropped it back on the bed. She felt a rush of anger. Courtney was fine. She'd called the sheriff twenty minutes ago. She must have seen Dakota's pickup parked in front of Zane's house from the county road.

Or she'd called so the sheriff would see Zane's scratched face.

"What are you up to, Courtney?" Dakota said to the empty bedroom. No good, that much she was sure of. "And what really happened here last night?"

The room provided few answers. Unless you read something into the crumpled sheets on the bed. She felt a surge of anger mixed with something she didn't want to admit. Jealousy. Zane had gone out with her sister.

I didn't want to hurt her feelings. She swore under her breath.

Too bad he hadn't felt that way when they were kids, Dakota thought, remembering how he'd pushed her away.

"You're just a kid," he'd said when she tried to hang around him at the rodeo grounds. "Go on. Find someone your own age to bug."

She ground her teeth at the memory. She'd had the worst crush on him. And, stupidly, she'd written it all down in her diary, every horrible tearful account, including her conviction: *Zane doesn't know it, but some day I'm going to marry him.*

Two days ago, when she'd realized that someone had been in her things, she'd discovered that her diary and some old photographs were missing. Courtney. She was the only one who could have taken the diary.

Now Dakota wondered when Courtney had taken it. Two weeks ago—about the same time that someone had mysteriously signed Zane Chisholm up for a dating service?

It was no coincidence that Courtney had tricked Zane into a date. Dakota was sure of that. Courtney had the diary. She knew how her sister had felt about Zane. So Courtney had done this out of meanness?

What had she hoped to accomplish by this? More than sibling rivalry, Dakota thought, remembering the scratches on Zane's face and the frantic phone call in the wee hours this morning.

Whatever Courtney was up to, Dakota was going to find her and put a stop to it. And Zane was going to help her.

Unlike him, Dakota had a bad feeling she knew exactly why Courtney had targeted him. She couldn't wait to get her hands on her diary—and her sister.

MRS. CROWLEY STEPPED into her room and closed the door firmly behind her. She had always been so good at playing her roles—she now thought of herself as Mrs. Crowley. Smiling at the thought, she locked the door to listen. She had to make sure she wouldn't be disturbed.

It hadn't taken long to learn the sounds of the house. The older section had more to say than the newer one, but she knew all of its many voices—which floorboards creaked, which doors opened silently, which spot in the house carried the most sound for eavesdropping.

She'd explored every square inch of the house until she knew she could move through it blind if she had to. That was a possibility if the house were ever to catch fire.

Satisfied that everyone was down for the night, she stretched, relieving her back from the strain of walking hunched over. She had taught herself to move silently and now chuckled to herself at how many times she'd been able to come up behind Emma without her knowing it and startle her.

Moving just as silently now, she stepped into the bathroom and studied herself in the mirror over the sink a moment before she reached up and took out the white contact lens. She blinked, waiting for the eye to focus. Then she removed the dark brown contact lens.

She slowly began to remove the burn scar, peeling it off as she peeled away Mrs. Crowley. At last she stood at the mirror, her face scrubbed clean, her eyes blue again.

As she stared at herself, though, she felt she was

looking at a stranger. It had been so long since she'd been herself, her image came as a shock.

But it was nothing compared to the shock it would give others in the house when the time came to end this charade, she thought with a wry smile.

Chapter Four

The moment Zane had gone into the bathroom and turned on the shower, he'd changed his mind about staying hidden while Dakota handled the sheriff.

He'd never run from trouble in his life, and he wasn't going to now. But as he'd reached for the bathroom door handle, he'd glimpsed his face again in the mirror over the sink. The scratches were an angry red and, maybe worse, he had no explanation for them.

Dakota was right. He needed to find Courtney and he couldn't do that behind bars. He feared anything he said to the sheriff would come out sounding like a lie. If Sheriff McCall Crawford saw Courtney's cell phone...

He'd stayed put even though it was hard. He couldn't hear what was being said. For all he knew, Courtney had been found and that was why the sheriff was here.

Zane jumped at the tap on the bathroom door. He quickly turned off the shower and opened the door.

"The coast is clear," Dakota said as he came out.

"What did McCall want?" He hated the fear he heard in his voice. From Dakota's reaction, she'd heard it too. She had to be wondering if she was wrong about him.

"Apparently Courtney called about a disturbance out here between you and me."

"*Courtney* called? Then she's all right?"

"Apparently."

He shook his head. "But why would she…" The thought struck him like a brick. "She wanted the sheriff to see the scratches on my face and arm. What the hell is going on with her?"

"She seems to have it in for the two of us," Dakota said. "That's why we have to find her and find out what she's up to."

"The *two* of us?"

Dakota looked away for a moment as if she hadn't meant to say that. "The last time I saw her was a few days ago. Right after that I realized she'd been in my house and taken something of mine." She waved a hand through the air. "The point is, I want it back. She had no business in my house, let alone taking anything of mine."

He nodded, seeing that whatever Courtney had taken, Dakota didn't want to talk about it. He changed the subject. "What did McCall make of all this?"

"She seemed to think it was my sister being jealous."

"We know better." The date last night, what he could remember of it, hadn't been anything special. In fact, he recalled before he'd lost his memory that he hadn't planned to see Courtney again. She was beautiful, but not that interesting.

His head still hurt, but a thought wormed its way through. "You said Courtney showed up two weeks ago. That's the same time someone broke into my house and used my computer to set up the rural dating account. Could she have been planning this that long ago, trying to set me up for more than a date?"

"Why go to the trouble?" Dakota asked, frowning as if she was trying to work it out herself.

"Why me at all?" It didn't make any sense to him either. "The requirements I put down for the perfect date apparently made Courtney the perfect match."

Dakota raised an eyebrow.

"I didn't put down *any* requirements, but whoever signed me up must have rigged it so that my requirements matched Courtney's. It had to be Courtney."

"A lot of trouble and to what end?"

"I guess that depends on what happened last night," he said as he glanced around the living room. Nothing seemed to be missing, but then he'd made that mistake before.

"You really don't remember what happened after your date?" she asked.

"I've never had a hangover like this before."

Dakota was looking at the scratches on his face again. "Maybe you should get a drug test at the hospital."

Dakota was willing to consider that he'd been drugged? Zane was surprised and relieved. But why hadn't he thought of it? Because he'd been running scared from the moment he'd opened his eyes this morning.

He had to know what he was dealing with. Courtney Baxter seemed to be setting him up. But why? He was just grateful that Dakota seemed to be on his side. If he'd just gotten drunk and didn't remember, that was one thing. But if Dakota was right and Courtney had drugged him...

"I think a drug test is a good idea," he said, but Dakota didn't seem to hear him.

She was looking at Courtney's cell phone. She had picked it up by two fingers. He could see the smeared blood from here.

"Any idea how it got blood on it?" she asked. "Or how it ended up under your bed? I noticed there was also a broken lamp on the other side of the bed. You probably don't know anything about that either."

He shook his head. "You said you heard something crash in the background when you were on the phone with her."

"Could have been the lamp." She looked down at the phone again. "Maybe we should see about getting DNA off this phone to find out if it is even Courtney's blood. We can have a doctor run a blood test on you at the same time for possible drugs. Do you have a small plastic sandwich bag we can put this in?"

"Top drawer on the right." He watched her head for the kitchen, trying to figure out what about Dakota was bothering him. She certainly was taking all this better than he would have thought.

"I doubt there will be fingerprints other than ours, but…" She stopped on her way back from the kitchen, the cell phone in a plastic bag she'd found in the drawer. "What's wrong?"

He wasn't sure. "You just kept me out of jail—at least temporarily—and now you're going to help clear me? What's going on, Dakota?"

"I told you. I need your help to find Courtney."

"Because she took something of yours that you want back. If you just wanted to find Courtney, you could have told the sheriff everything you know and thrown me to the wolves," he said. "The sheriff, with all her resources, would be looking for your sister right now.

So why didn't you? It wasn't just to keep me out of jail so I could help you find her. I hate to sound suspicious, but I have to wonder why you're so anxious to find her that you would throw in with *me*."

"She's my sister."

"Uh-huh."

Dakota sighed. "Okay, maybe I've suspected she was up to something from the first time I laid eyes on her."

"You said your father's name and signature are on her birth certificate. Are you saying you're questioning that?"

She shrugged. "All I know is that something's wrong with her story. After what you've told me, I'm even more convinced."

"But not enough to go to the sheriff."

"I want to do some investigating of my own before I get the sheriff involved," Dakota said.

He suspected there was more, something she was hiding, but right now he was just glad he wasn't in jail. "Then you believe me?"

"I'm willing to consider you were set up." She stepped to the door and opened it. "On the way into town, I think we should see who Courtney's been calling—and who's been calling her."

DAKOTA HADN'T BEEN completely truthful. Not that she didn't have her reasons for wanting to believe Zane and, if she was being honest with herself, some of them had to do with the crush she'd had on him when she was a girl.

He was even more handsome now. Not that she was the kind of woman who was overcome by good looks. Zane hadn't made fun of her like the other boys when she'd been the skinny, freckle-faced, buck-toothed, mouth-full-of-braces girl who'd hung around him like a lovesick puppy.

Nor was she that smitten girl anymore. But she also believed that Zane, while no longer the lanky boy she'd known as a girl, was still honorable and decent. She had to trust her instincts. Her instincts told her that Zane was telling the truth.

"I'll drive," she said, and Zane didn't argue. He looked like death warmed over, making her also believe she might be right about him having been drugged.

She could tell that his greatest fear was that something really awful had happened to Courtney last night. Dakota told herself it was more likely, after what the sheriff had said, that Courtney was up to her pretty little neck in this and not as the victim. Another reason Dakota wanted to find her as quickly as possible.

As she drove, she watched Zane out of the corner of her eye as he began to check the numbers on the cell phone through the plastic bag.

"There are no contact numbers," Zane said. "I get the feeling this is a fairly new phone, since there are so few calls and messages. The last outgoing call was…" He read off the number.

"That's the number at my ranch from when Courtney called last night. Do you recognize any of the other numbers?"

"As for incoming, there are calls and messages from you and Arlene Evans Monroe. I had asked her to call Courtney and get back to me when she heard from her." He studied the numbers for a moment. "Otherwise there are two incoming calls from numbers that I don't recognize. Courtney returned one of those calls, but not the most recent one."

Dakota realized she hadn't told Zane about the phone call earlier. "Someone was looking for her. Before the sheriff left your house, Courtney's cell phone rang. I answered it. I could hear breathing on the other end of the line, but the person didn't say anything before hanging up."

"Courtney? If she was the one who called the sheriff about a disturbance at my house," he said, his brows furrowing.

"Or someone else looking for Courtney."

"Do you recognize either of these numbers?" He read the numbers off to her.

"Sorry, they don't sound familiar. There's a notebook and pen in the glove box," she told him as they neared town.

Zane jotted down the numbers as Dakota pulled into the back of the hospital.

Whitehorse County Hospital was small. As they walked in the back door, Zane spotted Dr. Buck Carrey. He looked more like a rancher than a doctor. A big man, he had a weathered face wrinkled from the sun and from smiling. His gray hair was uncharacteristically long for Whitehorse and pulled back in a ponytail. Today he was wearing jeans, boots and a Western shirt, with his white Stetson cocked back on his head.

He greeted Zane warmly, then shook hands with Dakota, whom he hadn't had the pleasure of meeting before, and invited them into his office. "You said this was a confidential matter?" he asked, closing the door.

Dakota listened while Zane gave an abbreviated version of what they needed. Doc raised a brow when Zane showed him the phone. "Let's start with the blood test. As for the DNA, I need something to compare it to."

"I'm her sister. Well, half sister. Will that work?"

"Close enough." Doc left and came back with the items he needed to do both tests. He took blood from Zane, then a swab of Dakota's mouth and another swab of blood from the phone.

"I'll have to get back to you on your blood test," he told Zane. "Same with the blood on the phone." Doc seemed to study Zane's scratches for a moment. "You sure you don't want the sheriff in on this?"

"If we can't find Courtney, we'll go to the sheriff," Dakota promised. Her sister was in trouble, she'd bet on that. But she feared it was Courtney's own making.

"I'M SORRY ABOUT ALL THIS," Zane said as they left the hospital. "First your father's death, then a sister you never knew you had and now this."

Dakota shrugged as she opened her pickup door and slid behind the wheel. "I think what hurt the most was that I'd always wanted a sister and apparently I've had one since I was two—I just didn't know it."

"Why do you think your father kept it from you?"

She shook her head. "Guilt maybe. Everyone says he adored my mother, but when she got sick, I don't think he could handle it."

"I can't imagine your father living a double life, not the way he felt about your mother." He also couldn't imagine Clay Lansing keeping all of this from his daughter. There had to be more to the story. "So what do you know about Courtney's mother?"

"Nothing, really," Dakota said. "Courtney said she died and that she doesn't like to talk about it."

"Did she mention where she was raised, at least?"

"Great Falls. She wasn't even that far away, just a few hours. My father must have seen her when he went there, since she was at the hospital when he died."

"He died in Great Falls?" Zane asked in surprise.

Dakota nodded and seemed to concentrate on her driving. "All of it has come as such a shock—his death, Courtney, the lie he lived all these years." He could hear the hurt in her voice. "She had more time with him at the end than I did," Dakota said, voicing her pain.

"If she's telling the truth," Zane said as he looked over at her. "You suspected something about her story was a lie, didn't you?"

She glanced at him in surprise.

He smiled. "I know you, Dakota. You wouldn't have believed me so quickly if you didn't suspect your sister was up to something." True, they hadn't seen each other in years, but in so many ways she was that kid he knew from the rodeo grounds. She'd always seemed too smart for her own good.

"If you're right and you were set up, then Courtney is in on it," Dakota said. "I can't imagine any other reason she would sign up for Arlene's rural dating service. One look at her tells me she's never had trouble finding a date."

Zane had been one of those men. He cursed himself for it. "I need to see her room where she was staying."

"She's not there," Dakota said. "I checked and her car wasn't there before I came looking for you."

"She might have dumped her car somewhere."

"Why would she do that?"

He shook his head. "Why would she pretend we had a date and possibly drug me?"

"You don't know she was the one who signed you up for Arlene's rural dating service," Dakota pointed out.

"No, but she had to be in on it. That's the only thing that makes any sense. You didn't check to make sure she wasn't at home, a friend maybe had given her a ride home?"

Dakota shook her head. "She doesn't have any friends here."

"That you know of," Zane said. "Let's try her room first. If she set me up…"

"You think she's cleared out."

"Yeah, that's exactly what I'm thinking. I'm sure there's more, but I have a feeling this next part is her being scarce until the other shoe drops," he said.

THEY REACHED CHINOOK, a small, old town along the railroad, down the Highline from Whitehorse. She turned north on a dirt road toward the Lansing ranch, traveling through the rolling prairie.

It had been a clear blue day, the kind that are almost blinding. Now the sun had dipped behind the Bear Paw Mountains, the sky a silken blue-gray and still cloudless. A meadowlark sang a song that traveled along with them as she drove.

"You say she doesn't have any friends," Zane said as he watched the countryside roll by and tried to get a clear picture of what Courtney Baxter was really like. He couldn't shake the feeling that he hadn't been out with the "real" Courtney last night. "No one you've seen her with, no phone calls?"

Dakota shook her head.

"When I woke up and Courtney was gone, I just assumed she'd left on her own," he said. "But what if there'd been someone else with her at my house last night after I passed out?"

He felt her studying him again, stealing glances at him as she drove. "Dakota, you know me. I wouldn't have hurt her."

She let out a breath. "I know."

"Thank you for believing in me. I suspect whatever this is, Courtney isn't in it alone and I have a bad feeling your sister doesn't realize how dangerous the person she got involved with really is."

"Oh, I don't know about that. I get the feeling Courtney can take care of herself."

Dakota drove past the large old, white, single-story ranch house to the small matching guesthouse out back. Zane remembered when they were kids and Dakota had told him that her father had built a house on the ranch for her to stay in when she reached sixteen. He recalled her excitement because she was like him. She never wanted to leave the ranch; she just didn't want to live at home.

But something had changed for her to end up in New Mexico, engaged to a guy involved in investment managing.

Zane saw as they climbed out of the pickup that Courtney's compact car was nowhere in sight.

Dakota knocked at the front door. "Courtney?"

He held his breath, praying she would open the door. Dakota knocked again, then pulled out a key and opened the door.

As the door swung in, Zane caught the scent of perfume, the familiarity of it making him a little sick to his stomach and increasing his dread. What had happened last night? The harder he tried to remember, the worse he felt.

The guesthouse was small, one bedroom, one bath with a kitchenette and living area. The bedroom door was ajar. Dakota stepped over to it, carefully pushing the door all the way open to expose an empty, unmade bed.

"It doesn't look like she's been back," Dakota said as he headed over to the closet and eased the door open.

Only a handful of clothes hung there. He frowned and moved to the chest of drawers. The top drawer held a few undergarments. The next drawer had even less, only a couple of tank tops and pajama bottoms. The third drawer had two pairs of jeans, and the bottom drawer was empty.

He closed the last drawer and turned to look at Dakota. "What woman has so few clothes?"

She shrugged. "Maybe this is all she owns."

"Or maybe she left most of her belongings somewhere else. Does she have a job?"

"She said she's been looking locally."

He smiled at that. "Not looking very hard, right?"

Dakota sighed. "I got the feeling she was waiting for me to offer her half the ranch."

If Courtney Baxter really was Clay Lansing's love child, then she could probably legally force Dakota to split the ranch and the rough stock business with her. He swore under his breath. How could Clay have done this to Dakota? Worse, he'd kept her sister from her— and let Dakota learn about her after he was gone. Didn't he realize the repercussions of his actions?

Zane moved to the bed. A clock radio sat on one of the bedside tables, nothing else. He bent down to look under the bed and was hit again with the smell of Courtney's perfume. For a moment he thought he would be sick. He stilled his stomach and squinted into the darkness under the bed.

Something glinted. Reaching in, he felt the cool, weathered vinyl surface, found the handle and pulled the old suitcase from under the bed.

He glanced at Dakota.

"Maybe you'd better make sure it isn't ticking before you open it," she said.

He popped the latches on each side. The suitcase fell open.

EMMA CHISHOLM GLANCED OUT the window, surprised to see Mrs. Crowley silhouetted against the fading twilight.

Instinctively, Emma stepped back, afraid the woman might have seen her. She was relieved when she stole another glance and saw that Mrs. Crowley had her back to the house.

What was she doing out there? The woman never went outside. At least not that Emma had ever noticed.

Peering around the edge of the curtain, it took her a moment to realize the housekeeper was on a cell phone. Emma had never seen her make or take a call. No cell phone had ever rung while Mrs. Crowley was working. Emma was actually surprised that the housekeeper even owned one.

She couldn't help but wonder who the woman was talking to. Mrs. Crowley made it clear she had no one who would interfere with her ability to stay at the ranch and work every day except one each week.

When pinned down, the housekeeper had said she

was widowed, no children. She'd quickly made it clear she thought Emma had stepped over some invisible line by even asking.

"It could be a friend," Emma muttered to herself. But even as she said it, she had her doubts. "Maybe a friend from before the accident."

That was something else that Mrs. Crowley made clear she wasn't going to talk about.

"People don't just stare at me," she said, her voice sharp with bitterness and anger. "They want to know what happened. Like vultures, they would love to hear every horrible detail." Mrs. Crowley's one good eye glinted like granite. "Well, they won't be hearing it from me and neither will you."

With that, she'd turned and limped off.

Emma watched now from the edge of the curtain as Mrs. Crowley finished her phone call and stood for a long moment as if admiring what little remained of the sunset.

As she turned to come back to the house, her gaze rose to the second floor as though she sensed Emma watching her.

Emma jerked back, heart hammering. The last thing she wanted Mrs. Crowley to think was that she was spying on her, true or not.

After a moment, Emma dared to take another peek. Mrs. Crowley was still standing in the same spot. The harsh glow of the sunset fell across the woman's disfigured face. She was smiling her crooked half smile, her gaze mocking as she looked up at the second-floor window, making sure that Emma knew she'd been caught spying on her.

Chapter Five

Empty. The suitcase was empty? Dakota laughed, letting out the breath she'd been holding. She'd been so afraid of what they were going to find. "It's just an old suitcase. Looks like it belonged to another generation."

"Like her mother?" Zane said with the lift of an eyebrow.

"More like her grandmother." Dakota leaned over it and caught a whiff of stale air that reminded her of her own grandmother. "My nana had a similar suitcase. It even smelled a little like this one."

The suitcase had been expensive because it had been made to withstand even a fall from a plane, supposedly. She realized what Zane was getting at. These particular suitcases, because of their expense, often had the name and address of the owner engraved on a plate inside.

She peered into the silky lining. Her fingers brushed over something cold and slick at the edge. She looked up at Zane and smiled as her fingers found the engraving. Turning the suitcase to the light, she read, "Frances Dean, 212 W. River St., Great Falls, Montana."

"Don't get too excited. Your sister could have picked this suitcase up at a garage sale," Zane said.

"Or this could be a relative." As she started to pull her hand back from the metal tag, her fingers caught on the lining. It tore. When she looked down she saw why her fingers had caught. The lining appeared to have been cut.

"Well, would you look at that," Zane said as he peered into the space between the lining and the hard cover of the suitcase.

He reached in and drew out a thin stack of hundred-dollar bills.

Dakota felt her eyes widen. "Do you think Courtney knew the money was in there?"

Zane sent her an are-you-serious look. "Who do you think put this money in there? The bills are new."

"How much is it?" Dakota asked as he began to dig out the stacks.

"I'd say at least ten thousand."

Ten thousand dollars? "I don't understand this. Courtney let me think she was broke. She'd been borrowing money from me until she could find a job, she said."

Zane shook his head sympathetically. "Apparently your sister took us both in. Any idea where she might have gotten it?" He tossed the money into the suitcase, snapped it shut and grabbed the handle.

"Probably from whoever put her up to whatever no good she's involved in," she said, still in shock. Courtney had played them both. "You're taking the suitcase?"

He smiled. "Looks like we're going to Great Falls to find out if Frances Dean knows where we can find Courtney. In the meantime, we have the money. Which means it's only a matter of time before Courtney comes looking for *us*."

DAKOTA GLANCED AT HER WATCH. It was several hours to Great Falls. There was no way they would get there in time to talk to anyone—at least not tonight.

"Don't you think we should wait and go in the morning?" she asked.

He shook his head. "I'm afraid of what Courtney will do next if we wait. This way we can try to track down whoever lives at the address on the suitcase first thing in the morning. You don't have to come if you don't want to."

No chance of that. "Just let me go over to the house and throw a few things into a bag."

"Dakota," he said as she started to turn away. "Thank you. I'm glad you're in this with me."

She felt a stab of guilt. *Tell him about the diary. He needs to know that you're the one who involved him in this.*

"Give me ten minutes," she said, and hurried across the yard, telling herself that Courtney had to have more of a motive for involving Zane than sibling rivalry. Dakota hadn't even seen Zane in years.

But she realized as she packed a few items of clothing in an overnight bag that Courtney might be using Zane because she felt cheated. Maybe she thought she should have had everything Dakota had since she didn't get to live on the ranch with their father.

Who knows what made Courtney do what she has, let alone what she is planning to do next, Dakota thought. Zane wasn't the only one worried about that.

On impulse, Dakota went into her father's den. Once she'd realized that Courtney had been in the house and taken her old diary, she'd been so upset that she'd only given a cursory look for what else her sister might have taken.

Now she had a bad feeling as she went behind her father's desk and saw that the bottom drawer was partially open. There were gouges in the wood where someone had used something sharp to break the lock.

With trembling fingers, Dakota pulled the drawer out, knowing what had been inside was gone—and who had taken it.

ZANE FOUND DAKOTA standing in her father's study. He tried to read her expression, but the afternoon light cast her face in shadow.

"Is everything all right?" he asked.

She looked up and seemed surprised to see him, as if she'd forgotten about him. He figured she was thinking about her father, missing him. He regretted interrupting her but they had to get going.

"I hate to rush you—"

"You're not," she said quickly. "I'm ready."

He saw her overnight bag by the door and picked it up. "Anything else?"

She shook her head. She seemed distracted, but he didn't press her as they walked out to her pickup.

"I thought we'd go to my place if you don't mind. I can pack a few things and we can take my truck. I'm feeling much better."

"Whatever you think," she said. He could tell wherever her mind had been, it was still there.

They were both quiet on the drive back to his house. It wasn't until they were on the road to Great Falls that Dakota broke the silence.

"You think Courtney was paid to set you up?" she asked.

That's exactly what he thought. But ten thousand dollars? That was a lot of money. Way more money than he was worth setting up.

"I just can't understand why anyone might have paid your sister to do this," he said. "Especially that *much* money. And other than me looking like I got into a cat-fight and feeling hungover, what was the point? Unless she was supposed to kill me...."

"Don't say that. Even if Courtney drugged you, I'm sure she didn't mean to take it that far."

Zane looked over at Dakota. "I thought her phone call to you was part of the setup, but what if she really was in trouble? What if she *was* supposed to kill me and couldn't go through with it? That could explain why she's disappeared. She's hiding from whoever paid her to do the job."

"Why would she want you dead? And why didn't she come back for the money? Unless the money wasn't her real reason for what she did."

"That's why I don't think she acted alone. But it has to be someone with a grudge against me." He glanced over at Dakota and gave her a crooked grin. "As I recall, you had quite a temper when I riled you up. You out to get me, Dakota?"

"That's not funny." She turned away.

Zane stared out at the Montana evening as they drove through the rolling green prairie. This was such a beautiful time in this part of Montana. The mountain ranges were capped with pristine white snow from the last snowfall in the high country. The snow and deep blue mountains were in stark contrast to the lush green of the prairie. Creeks ran wild with the beginning of summer runoff and there was a feeling of new beginnings in the air.

It was the kind of evening he loved and yet he was too aware of the woman sitting just inches away from him.

Dakota didn't seem to be aware of him. Something was bothering her. But apparently it wasn't anything she wanted to share with him. He'd been joking earlier about her being a part of this. What if she was?

DAKOTA WAS FURIOUS with her half sister and couldn't wait to find her. If Courtney even really was her sister.

She'd been so shocked when she'd first learned about Courtney that she now realized she should have demanded more proof. All she'd had was a glance at Courtney's birth certificate. Once she'd seen her father's name and his signature…

Why hadn't she questioned that the birth certificate might have been a fake? She'd invited Courtney to come live at the ranch—a stranger. Now she regretted that terribly. What else had Courtney taken from the house? Dakota didn't know. Just as she didn't know why Courtney was doing this or what she had to gain other than possibly ten thousand dollars.

Dakota had put off telling Zane what she'd discovered missing in her father's den. She needed time to let all of this sink in so she could sort it out. At least that's what she told herself. But she hadn't sorted it out and Zane needed to know. He already suspected that Courtney was supposed to kill him last night. What if he was right? What if Courtney tried again?

"There's something I need to tell you," she said as

they left the meandering Milk River behind and headed south toward the Missouri—and the city of Great Falls. "I told you Courtney took something of mine."

"But you don't want to tell me what she took."

She knew it was silly not to confess about the diary. But she was embarrassed by all the things she'd written. With luck, she would get it back and Zane would never have to know.

Letting out a breath, she said, "Courtney took some old photos along with a pistol my father kept in the bottom drawer of his desk. It's a .45."

Zane let out a curse. "You're just now telling me about this?"

"I didn't check until I went in to pack for this trip. But after everything that has happened…"

"Wait," he said, holding up a hand. "You came looking for her because of something she took, right? Something that had you upset enough that you actually believed I had been set up."

"Courtney had also taken some personal things of mine, including some old photographs."

"Old photographs?"

"Some of my father at several rodeos and one of you and me."

He blinked at her. "She took a gun and a photo of your father and one of the two of *us?*"

"I'm sorry. I should have told you."

"You think she *targeted* me because of a photograph of the two of us? That's why you believed me! That's why you're so anxious to find her and why you didn't want the sheriff involved." He shot her a look, then laughed. "Dakota, you aren't responsible for this. Seriously. You can't believe that's all that's behind this."

She shook her head, feeling close to tears.

He grinned. "You had a photo of the two of us?"

She brushed at the tears. "It was a good one of *me*. You just happened to be in the picture," she said, and looked away, but she knew he was still grinning. Just as she knew he was wrong. She *was* responsible somehow for what was happening.

EMMA CHISHOLM HEARD the steady throb of an engine and slipped out of bed. At the window, she saw one of the ranch pickups pull around to the side of the house. She glanced back at the clock beside the bed. 2:11 a.m.

As the driver cut the engine, she thought it must be one of her six stepsons. But since they each had their own homes it would be unusual for one of them to come by this late—unless there was trouble.

Emma was surprised when Mrs. Crowley stepped from the pickup.

"I will need a vehicle at my disposal," Mrs. Crowley had announced the day she'd appeared at their door. "I'd prefer not to drive my own car given the condition of your…rural roads."

Emma had to shoot Hoyt a warning look to keep him from saying what she knew he was thinking.

"There is always a ranch pickup around. Will that do?" Emma had asked the woman. She was determined to make this work, one way or the other.

Mrs. Crowley had turned her nose up, but said that would have to do.

"Who the hell does she think she is?" Hoyt had demanded later when the two of them had gone out to the barn. That was where they escaped to, knowing that Mrs. Crowley wouldn't set foot out there. "If you knew what I was paying her…" He'd broken off, looking chagrined.

"It's all right. I know she didn't come cheap." Emma appreciated that he'd gone to so much trouble to make sure she was safe. She knew that Hoyt would pay any price for her safety.

"Yeah, well, the problem is that no one wants to work for a murderer. Even an acquitted one."

"Stop that," Emma had snapped. "The problem is that no one wants to be more than a mile from a mall." She'd laughed. "They just don't realize that there isn't a mall anywhere that can beat being out here."

Hoyt had smiled as he'd cupped his hand behind her neck and pulled her close. "How did I get so lucky with you?"

Emma could have told him, since he was the sexiest man she'd ever known and the biggest-hearted. Any woman would have been a fool not to love this man and appreciate the land that he loved. But she'd bit back her words. His first wife, Laura, hadn't appreciated either.

Now Emma wondered what Mrs. Crowley was doing out at this time of night. She didn't seem like the type of person to close down the bars in Whitehorse, but as secretive as she was, who knew her type?

The woman reached back into the pickup cab for the large purse she carried. It was more like a carpetbag, and tonight it seemed fuller than ever. What did Mrs. Crowley carry in there, anyway?

With a start, Emma realized that the woman could have a secret life at night. It wasn't the first time she'd taken off after supper without a word. She could have come in late all those nights as well and Emma just hadn't heard her before.

Still, as she watched Mrs. Crowley carefully close the pickup door so as not to disturb anyone and then disappear into the lower floor of the house, Emma was amazed at the woman's stamina. As hard as she worked, refusing even a break, how could she stay out this late and still be up before the sun in the morning?

On her day off, Mrs. Crowley stayed in her room, not even interested in food. Everything about the woman was a mystery to Emma. The weather was beautiful this time of year and yet she showed no interest in the land right outside her window. In fact, the drapes on her windows were always closed.

Maybe the sunlight bothered her burned skin and eye, Emma thought, chastising herself for finding fault with the woman. Mrs. Crowley had made it possible for Hoyt to return to work with his sons. No more babysitting Emma day after day.

Emma stepped back from the window, telling herself it was none of her business. Climbing back into bed beside Hoyt, she snuggled closer. It didn't matter what the woman did late at night or on her day off in her room.

But Emma had a terrible time getting back to sleep. What did they really know about the woman who lived in their house with them?

Zane frowned as he took in the house. The house at 212 W. River Street was a narrow, two-story wood structure that had once been white before all the paint had peeled off. Like the neighborhood, it had an abandoned look.

He glanced over at Dakota. They hadn't said much since he'd knocked on her motel door to see if she was ready for breakfast. Last night when they had stopped at a motel, it had felt awkward.

He'd stopped thinking of her as a kid and that was part of the problem. She seemed embarrassed and clearly hated admitting that she'd kept a picture of the two of them from when she'd had a crush on him. He couldn't help being flattered that she'd kept it. He'd always pretended to his friends that Dakota hanging around bugged him. But he'd been sorry when her father had moved his rough stock part of the ranch to New Mexico and Dakota had gone with it.

Right now, he was glad that they had that history together. True, she had her reasons for wanting to find her sister, but he doubted she would have believed him about Courtney otherwise. Just as he was sure she wouldn't have wanted his help if she didn't somehow feel responsible.

But Zane didn't believe that Courtney Baxter had come after him because of some photo she'd seen of the two of them from years ago. If Courtney wanted to hurt Dakota, the best way was to try to take Lansing Ranch. Not only would it kill Dakota to lose it, the ranch was worth a lot of money, not to mention the rough stock business. Worth a lot more than ten thousand dollars.

The question still remained though: Why come after *him?* What was to be gained other than the money?

The money alone meant Courtney hadn't come up with this by herself. He suspected Dakota was right about the phone call from her sister. Maybe Courtney really had been scared and crying out for help. Or maybe that had been part of the setup. Maybe Courtney wanted to throw the two of them together. He felt foolish this morning for ever suspecting Dakota.

Now, as they climbed out of his pickup, he feared the address they'd found in the suitcase was a dead end.

He'd hoped the name plaque might lead them somewhere, but it appeared the house was empty and had been for some time.

Everything around the house was overgrown to the point that the vegetation was slowly taking over the structure. No one had lived here in a very long time.

"Hello?" The voice was small, just like the woman whose head barely topped the fence between the properties. "Can I help you?" the neighbor asked.

She had a shock of white hair that seemed to float like a halo around her head. Dressed in worn blue overalls, a red long-sleeved shirt and tennis shoes, the woman stepped out from behind the fence. She surveyed them with keen blue eyes. In her hands was a hedge trimmer.

"You live next door?" Zane asked, unable to hide his surprise. He'd thought for sure that the entire neighborhood was abandoned.

"Have for almost ninety years," she said proudly. "I was born here. But you're not looking for me, are you?"

"We were looking for Frances Dean," Dakota said, stepping forward.

"Dead, I'm afraid," the woman said. "Entire neighborhood's been dying off for years now. I'm about the only one left. A developer is just waiting for me to die so he can tear down what houses haven't fallen down and build a bunch of condos."

From her tone it was clear she was holding out until her last breath. "You aren't with that low-life vulture, are you?"

"No," Dakota assured her. "Did you know Frances Dean well?"

"All my life."

"Did she happen to have a daughter?" Zane asked.

"Camilla," the woman said with a nod. "Married one of the Hugheses. Widowed, I'd heard. Nice girl."

"Do you know if she has a daughter by the name of Courtney?" Dakota asked.

"Can't say. Last I heard of Frances she was worried because Camilla was having trouble getting pregnant." The old woman shrugged. She eyed Zane's scratches. "You look like you tangled with a rosebush. Did that once. Nasty thorns on those little devils."

"Well, thank you for your time, Mrs...."

"Miss. Abigail Warden." They introduced themselves. "Pleased to meet you. I suppose I should ask why you're looking for Frances's kin."

"A woman named Courtney Baxter has gone missing. We're trying to find her mother and we have reason to believe she might be related to Frances Dean," Dakota said.

"Might be. Might not. Good luck to you." Miss Warden turned back to the hedge with her clippers. As they left, they heard the *snap, snap, snap* of her blades.

"You know they're going to find that poor old woman under that hedge someday," Dakota said.

"There are worse ways to go," Zane said as they got back into the pickup. When his cell phone rang he pulled it out of his jacket pocket, hoping it was Courtney.

"It's Doc," he said to Dakota, then snapped open the phone. "Hello?"

"I got back your blood test," Doc said. "There were a variety of drugs in your system."

"One that would cause memory loss?"

"Several that would. You're lucky that mix of drugs didn't kill you."

Maybe it was supposed to. "What about the DNA on the phone?"

"I put a rush on it. We can get a basic preliminary test within twenty-four hours, so we should be hearing soon."

Zane thanked him and hung up, more upset than he wanted Dakota to know. Her sister had targeted him. To what end, he couldn't imagine. In fact, knowing what he did now, he was surprised he hadn't heard from Courtney. He wouldn't have put some sort of blackmail past her.

Of course, there was another option. That the reason Courtney hadn't turned up was because of whoever had put her up to this. Someone she hadn't trusted entirely and that's why she'd taken the gun from Clay Lansing's desk drawer. It made sense—if Courtney had feared she was going to need it.

Chapter Six

At a convenience store, Dakota borrowed a phone book. There were a half dozen Hugheses in the book, but only one C. Hughes. She jotted down the address, opting not to call first.

Fortunately, when they arrived at the address, there was a car in the driveway.

The first thing Dakota noticed about Camilla Hughes when she answered the door was how little she looked like Courtney. Camilla was a petite woman in her late fifties with dark brown hair and eyes. There was a cultured softness to both her manner and her speech. Again nothing like Courtney.

"May I help you?" Camilla asked, looking from Dakota to Zane and back.

"Hi, we're friends of Courtney's, just passing through town and we were hoping she might be around," Dakota said.

"Oh, I'm so sorry," Camilla said. "Courtney isn't here. Did she tell you she was going to be here?"

Dakota stole a look at Zane, pleased that she'd been right about the suitcase. Still, Courtney's lack of resemblance to this woman worried her. That and the fact that their last names were different.

"No," Dakota said. "Since we were in town we thought we'd just take the chance that she might be."

"Have you tried calling her?" Camilla asked.

"I'm not sure I have her number with me," Dakota said.

"Come in." Camilla waved them into her spotless, well-furnished home. "I'll get it for you." She went to a small desk just off the living room. As she was writing a number down for them on a notepad, Dakota moved to the fireplace.

There was a line of framed family photographs along the mantel. Dakota picked one up and turned it so Zane could see the woman in the studio shot. It was the same woman who'd showed up at Dakota's father's funeral, the same one Zane had taken to dinner last night. Courtney Baxter.

The other photographs were all of Camilla, a tall slim man with red, thinning hair and beautiful Courtney at various ages over the years. Dakota put the photo back on the mantel as Camilla Hughes came over to hand her the piece of notepaper.

The cell phone number Camilla had written down was different from the phone they'd found under Zane's bed. *Was that phone even Courtney's?* she wondered with surprise.

"Your name is Hughes but your daughter goes by Baxter?" Zane asked, expressing what Dakota had been wondering.

All the color washed from Camilla Hughes's face in an instant. She took a couple of steps to the side and lowered herself into a chair. "That's the name she's going by?"

He nodded, and Dakota could see that like her, he

was surprised that the woman had become so upset. As Camilla waved Zane into a seat across from her, Dakota joined him on the couch. "I'm sorry. I didn't know she was doing that. Baxter was her biological mother's name."

"She's *adopted?*" Dakota asked, unable to contain her surprise even with the obvious difference in appearance between mother and daughter. It explained why Courtney didn't resemble either her mother or father, though. But then Courtney didn't resemble their father or Dakota either. That meant she must have taken after her mother. Her *biological* mother?

"Yes, Marcus and I adopted her when she was only a few days old," Camilla said, still looking shaken.

"Her mother couldn't keep her?" Dakota had to ask, wondering about the mystery woman who'd had an affair with her father.

Camilla looked even more upset. "A nurse told me in private that the mother didn't want her, wanted nothing to do with her." Camilla instantly bit her tongue. "I've never told Courtney that, of course. I shouldn't have told you either. I'm just upset that Courtney has chosen to go by a woman's name who didn't want her."

"It's all right," Zane said. "I'm sorry this news has upset you so."

"Courtney has always known she was adopted, but she never seemed to have any interest in finding her birth parents," Camilla said. "I didn't even know that she knew her birth mother's last name." She seemed to shake herself out of her thoughts. "I'm sorry, but how is it that you know my daughter?"

Dakota felt telling Camilla about her relationship to Courtney would upset the woman further. Not to mention finding the ten thousand dollars tucked in the suitcase and the fact that her daughter seemed to be missing.

"We only recently met her," Dakota said. "Your daughter has been staying with me up north of Chinook."

"Staying with *you?*" Camilla asked, frowning.

"In my guesthouse. When we met, she said she needed somewhere to stay until she could find a job and get a place of her own," Dakota said.

Camilla shook her head in obvious bewilderment. "A few weeks ago she told me she was going on a short trip. She came over and borrowed her grandmother's suitcase. I haven't heard from her since and she hasn't been answering her phone...." She frowned. "If she's been staying up north, then why were you looking for her here?"

"She didn't come home the last two nights," Dakota said. "We were coming to Great Falls and thought she might be here. I wanted to let her know that a man at one of the jobs she'd applied for wanted to do a second interview."

She hated lying but the explanation seemed to relieve Camilla a little—that is, until she took a good look at Zane's scratched face.

"Rosebushes," Dakota said.

"Are there any high school friends or college friends she might be staying with?" Zane asked.

"She really hasn't been in touch with any of them that I know of." Camilla looked close to tears. "They all have jobs. Courtney was still trying to figure out what she wanted to do." She pursed her lips. Dakota could tell that she hated telling complete strangers such personal information. She only did so because of her obvious concern for her adopted daughter.

"Is it possible one of her birth parents contacted *her?*" Dakota asked.

Camilla seemed surprised by the question. "I hadn't thought of that. Maybe that's where she is now." She brightened at the thought. "Now that you mention it, Courtney hasn't been herself lately. She's been distant, secretive. I thought it was just growing pains, a sign that she wanted to be more independent from me."

"You said 'lately,'" Zane asked. "The past few weeks?"

Camilla nodded. "She even purchased a second cell phone a couple weeks ago. I thought that was odd. Clearly she didn't want me to know who she was calling—or who was calling her. I thought it might be a young man she wasn't ready to tell me about."

"Do you have that number?"

She shook her head. "She said she needed space. We've always been so close. Marcus and I spoiled her, no doubt about that. But maybe we should have pushed her out of the nest sooner. Then after Marcus died...I know I leaned on Courtney more than I should have."

"What about Courtney's birth father?" Dakota asked, trying to keep the emotion out of her voice.

Camilla shook her head. "The nurse I talked to didn't know anything about him."

"Isn't his name on the birth certificate?" Zane asked.

"No. Courtney's birth certificate shows my name and Marcus's."

"I'm confused," Dakota said. "Where was Courtney born?"

"It was a home birth somewhere in Montana. We got

a call. We didn't even realize that anyone knew how much we wanted a child and hadn't been able to have one of our own." She looked worried now. "It wasn't through an adoption agency exactly."

The Whitehorse Sewing Circle, Dakota thought. That group of old women had been secretly orchestrating adoptions for years. "Did your daughter get a quilt shortly after she was born?"

"Why, yes," Camilla said.

"So you don't know the names of her birth parents?" Zane asked.

"Just the mother's name. Lorraine Baxter."

Dakota recalled now that she had only glanced at the mother's name on the birth certificate that Courtney had shown her. It could have been Lorraine Baxter.

"You never tried to find her then?" she asked.

"Good heavens, no! That's why I was shocked when you told me that Courtney was going by the woman's name. You must be right about the woman contacting her. But why now? She didn't want her when she was born, why would she contact her now?"

Dakota knew there could be all kinds of reasons. She feared, though, given what they now knew, the reason wasn't a good one.

"When she picked up the suitcase, she didn't say where she was going?" Zane asked.

"No. That was something else that worried me. She said she had something she needed to do." Camilla's voice broke and tears welled in her dark eyes. "When she left, she hugged me and told me how much she loved me. But I had the most horrible feeling that she wasn't ever coming back, that she was telling me goodbye."

ZANE COULD SEE THAT DAKOTA was upset as they left. She'd promised to let Camilla know if they heard anything from Courtney.

"That poor woman," Dakota said as they climbed back into the pickup. "What if something bad has happened to my sister?"

"If she *is* your sister," Zane said.

Dakota frowned. "Courtney offered to take a DNA test anytime I wanted, but I didn't see any reason since she'd already showed me the birth certificate with my father's name and signature."

"I suspect that birth certificate could be a fake."

"I'm not sure how the Whitehorse Sewing Circle operates. But wouldn't there be an original birth certificate with the birth parents' names on it?"

He shrugged. "Maybe. If the mother thought she was going to keep the baby, then changed her mind, and the women of the Whitehorse Sewing Circle found the Hugheses, who were ready to adopt the baby, and saw that another birth certificate replaced the first. You heard what she said about the quilt. The Circle makes every baby it handles a quilt."

"If the mother didn't want the baby, then why would she keep the original birth certificate?" Dakota asked.

"Maybe she thought it would come in handy someday."

"Those women in the Circle have placed a lot of babies illegally and gotten away with it. If Courtney was my father's daughter then she was probably born somewhere near Whitehorse. Anyone with relatives or friends in Great Falls could have known about the Hugheses and their desire for a baby."

Zane nodded. "Your father would have known about

the Whitehorse Sewing Circle, which means that Courtney's mother would have probably known as well."

"Or maybe he sent her to the women so she could get rid of the baby," Dakota said.

"You know your father would never have done that."

"Do I? What if it was a woman he never should have gotten involved with?"

"A married woman?"

"Possibly."

Zane shook his head. "We won't know until we find Lorraine Baxter." He started the truck engine and drove, wondering where to go next. "This birth certificate Courtney showed you, did you ask Courtney for a copy?"

"I was so shocked I didn't ask for anything. But why put his name on the birth certificate if he isn't involved in this?"

Zane shot her a look. Was she serious? "He had money, a ranch, a good business."

"Still, Lorraine Baxter would have had to know him. She had to get a copy of his signature if she was going to forge his name. She didn't just pick his name out of thin air."

"Okay, let's say she knew him. Maybe had been intimate with him. Maybe Courtney *is* your half sister. The only way we're ever going to know everything is if we can find this woman. Don't look so skeptical," he said, glancing over at her. "If we're right, she's been in contact with Courtney and recently."

Dakota smiled at him. "You amaze me."

"Really?" he asked, grinning at her.

"You're a lot smarter than you look."

He had to laugh because he knew how he looked

with his face scratched up. He really wanted to find Courtney and get some answers, Dakota's sister or not.

"We need to try the numbers we found on her phone," he said.

"It might not even be Courtney's phone."

"Or it could be the extra phone she bought."

"So Courtney could talk to her birth mother without Camilla knowing about it," Dakota said.

"You're pretty sharp yourself," he joked as he pulled over. No reason to keep driving when they didn't have a clue where to go next.

He shut off the engine and turned to look at Dakota. He still wasn't used to the woman she'd grown into—or his reaction to her. He felt so close to her and yet they hadn't been around each other in years.

"Courtney must have gotten the birth certificate from her biological mother," Dakota said, frowning. "How else could Courtney have known about her birth father? Her adoptive mother didn't know his name and, apparently, neither did the nurse who delivered Courtney."

"If the birth mother was telling the truth and your father is really Courtney's father, then I doubt he ever knew he had a second daughter," Zane said. "I spent a lot of time around your father when I was rodeoing. Your father adored you. I can't believe he didn't have plenty of room for another daughter in his heart. He wouldn't have kept her a secret, and he wouldn't have given her up for adoption."

Her eyes filled with tears. "I want to believe that. I know he had wanted more children. If my mother hadn't gotten sick…"

Zane saw the pain behind the tears. She had hated

the thought that Clay had kept Courtney from her. Dakota had idolized her father. He'd been everything to her even before her mother died. To have a sister sprung on her like this must have been more painful for her than he could imagine.

But if Courtney really was the daughter of Clay Lansing, then her mother had had an affair with him either while his wife was dying of cancer or right after.

Zane just hoped the whole thing was a scam and that Courtney Baxter shared no blood ties with Dakota.

Dakota reached over and took his hand. "Thank you," she said, her voice breaking. "I've been struggling with this for weeks. I hated that I was suspicious of Courtney and I've been so angry with my father for keeping it from me."

Zane squeezed her hand. Leaning toward her, he drew her into his arms. He hadn't planned to kiss her. But at that moment, it seemed the most natural thing in the world.

Her lips parted, her breath warm and sweet. He felt a quiver run through her; his pulse kicked up as his mouth dropped to hers.

Dakota gently pushed him away. "Sorry, but your reputation precedes you."

He heard the slight tremble in her voice. She pulled free of his arms and he leaned back, telling himself he shouldn't have kissed her. Especially given why they were together. Didn't he have enough woman problems right now?

"You're going to believe rumors about me?" he joked as he tried to cover up how even that quick kiss had affected him.

She smiled, but there was hurt in her gaze. "Let's

not forget that you went out with a woman who simply showed up at your door."

"Yeah," he said, sobered by the memory. And not just any woman. Possibly Dakota's half sister. "You make a good argument." His gaze caressed her face for a moment before meeting her eyes. "But that kiss? I was just fulfilling a promise I made you before you moved to New Mexico. Remember?"

DAKOTA FELT HER FACE HEAT with embarrassment. Oh, she remembered all right.

"Don't you want to be the first boy I ever kiss?"

Zane looked down at her, sympathy in his gaze. "Your first kiss should be with someone special."

"That's why I want it to be with you." Her voice cracked, her eyes filling with tears. "I'm moving away and if you don't kiss me..."

"Dakota." He touched her shoulder, crouching down so that they were at eye level. His voice was soft. "That's real sweet, but there are going to be so many boys who want to kiss you. Boys you're going to want to kiss, too."

"Then will you at least save a kiss for me?"

Zane nodded and smiled, the caring look in his eyes making her love him all the more.

"Promise me that you'll kiss me one day. Promise?"

"I promise."

"I was just a silly kid," she said now.

"Yeah, you were. But you aren't anymore, are you? And I'm not sorry about the kiss."

Courtney's cell phone rang—the one they'd found under Zane's bed and at least believed was hers.

The sound startled Dakota and yet she'd never been

so glad for the interruption. She had wanted Zane Chisholm to kiss her since she was that silly kid who hung around him at the rodeo grounds.

But the phone was a good reminder that Zane had been with her sister two nights ago. She knew his reputation, and while she'd thrown herself at him when she was a girl and he was a teenager, she was no longer that starry-eyed tomboy. And Zane was definitely not that still-innocent teenager.

As for the kiss… Dakota told herself that as nice as it had been, it was just a kiss. But the purring of her pulse beneath her skin, the erratic beat of her heart, the quick breaths, all of those spoke of the true effect that Zane Chisholm's kiss had on her.

Dakota only hoped Zane hadn't noticed. Or if he had, that he thought it was the phone ringing that made her hand tremble as she pulled the bagged phone out of her purse.

She looked down at the phone as it rang again. "It's the same number calling from before, the one that hung up when I answered. What should I do?"

The phone rang a fourth time. "Don't answer it. Maybe they'll leave a message."

The phone rang once more, then fell silent.

SHERIFF MCCALL CRAWFORD stood in front of the mirror, studying her changed figure.

"It's beautiful. *You're* beautiful," her husband, Luke, said as he came up behind her and placed his palms over her bare, round abdomen. He kissed her on the back of the neck, then peeked at her in the mirror.

"Why are you frowning?" he asked.

"Was I?" she asked, quickly checking her expression. "I'm just so…big. I'm going to have to get a new uniform."

"Or you could go ahead and take maternity leave," Luke suggested.

She met his gaze in the mirror. "I have another month before the baby's due." She wasn't telling him anything he didn't already know. McCall turned in his arms to face him. "You want me to quit."

"No, I…" He sighed. "I just don't want anything to happen to you and the baby. I know that is horribly selfish. Sorry. It's just how I feel."

She started to tell him that she was the sheriff and had a job to do and that he knew that when he married her, but she stopped herself. She had to admit that lately she'd been feeling the same way.

She would be out on a call and feel their baby move inside her and all she could think about was that little life. The thought of putting their baby in jeopardy scared her. She didn't want to be afraid to do her job. If that happened, she told herself she would quit.

"Nick will be back in a few days." Her undersheriff would be filling in while she was on maternity leave. "I'll see about taking my leave then."

What she couldn't tell Luke was about her fears. Ruby hadn't been a bad mother, just not a great one. McCall wanted to be a great one.

But that was only one of her fears. She was afraid that she wouldn't want to go back to being sheriff after their daughter was born, that she had worked this hard to be the best law enforcement officer she could only to give it up. She felt torn and hated that feeling. Why couldn't she have it all?

Her cell phone rang.

Luke groaned. "Duty calls."

She kissed him and reached for her phone, listened, then said, "I'll be right there."

As she snapped the phone shut and reached to put on her clothing she saw her husband's expression. "A lime-green compact was found south of town in a ravine," she told him. "I'm sure there is nothing for you to look so worried about."

But as she climbed into her patrol SUV and headed south toward the isolated wilderness of the Missouri Breaks, McCall had a bad feeling about the car and driver.

The deputy had told her the car was registered to a Courtney Hughes. But in the purse found inside, he'd discovered a credit card under the name Courtney Baxter—the woman who'd been seen out with Zane Chisholm two nights ago.

McCall hated to jump to conclusions. But neither Zane Chisholm nor Courtney Baxter had called her back, she reminded herself as she drove the narrow dirt road south into the rugged breaks country.

Chapter Seven

"The caller didn't leave a message," Dakota said after checking. She couldn't help being disappointed, though not surprised.

"If Courtney left that phone under my bed on purpose—"

"Then that was probably her calling before to see if you'd found it," Dakota said.

"If she didn't, then someone else is looking for her. Might as well try the numbers she called and received calls from."

Dakota punched in the last number that had called.

The phone rang four times and went to voice mail. An electronic voice instructed her to leave a message.

She didn't.

She tried the only other different number. A male voice answered on the second ring.

"Where the hell are you?" the man demanded. "You leave in the middle of the night without a word? And what the hell am I supposed to do with your bar tab? If you think I'm picking it up, you're crazy."

Dakota looked over at Zane wide-eyed and mimed, "What do I do?"

"Talk?" he mouthed back.

She opened her mouth, but feared the man would hang up the moment she spoke. She let out a sigh, an impatient one like she'd heard Courtney do numerous times.

Silence.

"You're in trouble, aren't you?" he said, then swore angrily. "I told you not to get involved with these people." *These people?* Silence. "Courtney?"

"You were right," Dakota said, dropping her voice in the hopes she would sound enough like her sister.

Silence. Then he let out a curse. She heard the telltale sound of the phone disconnecting.

"Well," she said after repeating what the man had said, "Courtney's involved in something."

"Yeah, we kind of figured that. Bar tab, huh? Would you recognize the man's voice if you heard it again?"

"I think so."

"Sounds like she hooked up with a bartender at one of the local bars and ran up a tab," Zane said. "We might have to hit the bars."

Dakota nodded as she looked down at the list of phone numbers. "No other numbers we don't know."

THE LIME-GREEN COMPACT CAR was almost hidden in a stand of old junipers at the bottom of the ravine.

McCall found her deputy waiting for her beside a patrol car parked at the side of the road. As she walked over to the edge of the ravine, she noted the tire tracks where the car had gone off the road.

"No skid marks, no sign of the driver trying to brake," the deputy said as he joined her.

"Could have been going too fast and missed the curve, didn't have time to brake," McCall said.

"Yep, could have," he agreed.

That was, if Courtney Baxter had been driving the car.

"Got to wonder what she was doing way out here," the deputy said.

"No sign of the driver?" McCall asked.

The deputy shook his head. "I couldn't find any tracks, but then we had that big storm down this way the other night. Could have covered 'em."

"Let's go see," McCall said, and saw the deputy shoot her a look.

"It's pretty steep," he warned.

She ignored him and started down the slope. It *was* steep, the ground unstable. The dirt moved under her, an avalanche of soil. She began to slide and realized too late how she'd let her pride overrun her good sense.

Fortunately, the embankment ended at the edge of the junipers. She slid to a stop near the bottom of the ravine, grabbed a branch on one of the juniper trees and used it to keep from sliding any farther.

She felt the baby kick and smiled. That had actually been fun, she thought as she moved around the junipers to the side of the lime-green vehicle.

One glance told her what she already knew. The car was empty.

McCall glanced around, checking the ground for footprints. The only ones in the dirt were the deputy's. Either he was right about the storm erasing them, or no one had been in the car when it had gone off the road.

McCall pulled on the latex gloves from her pocket and opened the driver's side door. She caught the smell of something sour and felt her stomach roil. She'd been this way since the beginning of her pregnancy. No three months of morning sickness for her. Every smell affected her.

As she drew back from the odor, she noticed that the keys were in the ignition and the car was in Neutral. She checked the seat. It was pushed all the way back.

Whoever had last driven this car was long-legged, possibly longer-legged than Courtney Hughes aka Courtney Baxter.

McCall suspected that someone had pushed the car off the road into the deep ravine. Hoping it wouldn't be found?

Hard to hide a lime-green anything, though.

Holding her breath, she leaned into the car to check under the seats. She found the bloody rag stuffed under the passenger seat. It was wrapped around something heavy. Carefully, she turned back the dark-stained edges of the rag to reveal a gun.

The grip was stained with what appeared to be blood. The smell of the dried blood turned her stomach. She quickly wrapped the gun back up, leaving it on the floor of the passenger side, and stepped away from the car.

Taking large gulps of fresh air, McCall fought to keep her breakfast down. The last thing she wanted to do was contaminate the scene. She took a few more deep breaths, steadied herself, then called to the deputy to contact the state crime lab.

After a few moments, she made the climb back up to her patrol SUV. The baby kicked again. She placed her hand on her stomach, felt the movement and made a promise to her infant and her husband that she would stop this—as soon as the undersheriff got back. Just a few more days.

"Everything is going to be fine," she whispered as much to herself as her baby.

But she feared that wasn't the case for Courtney Baxter.

DAKOTA DROVE PART OF THE WAY back to the Lansing ranch while Zane slept.

She'd had a lot of time to think. Too much time apparently, since she'd found herself reliving Zane's kiss. A part of her wished she hadn't cut it off when she had. Another part of her, the logical, smart part, thought she should have stopped him sooner.

She was more than aware of Zane's reputation with women. She had no intention of becoming one of them. Last night, lying in her motel room bed, knowing he was only feet away in the next room, she'd had a terrible time getting to sleep.

Dakota hated that he still had that effect on her. She felt like that silly girl who'd trailed after him hoping for even just a smile from him.

As she turned down the road to the ranch, she knew she couldn't keep spending day after day with him.

Zane jerked awake as she pulled into the yard and cut the engine. Without a word, he was out of the pickup and striding toward the front door of the guesthouse.

She went after him. "Courtney's car isn't— Just a minute. I have the key…." Her words died off as she saw Zane try the knob. It turned in his hand and the door swung open.

He glanced back at her, all his fears culminating in his expression. He seemed to brace himself as he waited for her to join him before he stepped inside.

Dakota wasn't sure what she expected. She had a

pretty good idea that Zane might have anticipated finding Courtney sprawled dead on one of the Navajo rugs gracing the hardwood floors.

The small living area was empty. So were the kitchen and bedroom and bath, as well as the closet.

"She's cleared out," Zane said, turning to look at her.

Dakota stared at the empty closet in surprise. When Courtney had shown up at their father's funeral with evidence that she was her half sister, Dakota had been afraid Courtney was after half the ranch.

After the shock of having a sister had worn off, Dakota had decided that Courtney deserved half interest in the ranch and their father's business. She was Clay Lansing's daughter, after all, and she'd missed out on a lot. Why shouldn't she have a chance to live on the ranch if she wanted to?

"I always wanted a sister," she said.

Zane gave her an odd look.

"I was just getting used to the idea." She sighed. "She would have noticed that her suitcase and money were missing, don't you think?"

"Unless she wasn't the one who cleaned everything out. Whoever gave her the money might not know what she did with it."

"Why would someone else remove all her things?"

"To make us think she is still alive."

Still alive. Dakota felt a chill at his words.

"If Courtney came back and realized her suitcase was missing, I'm sure she'll be in contact with you soon." He didn't sound as if he believed that was going to happen any more than she did.

She watched him search the small guesthouse. "What are you looking for?"

"Anything she might have left behind. You didn't happen to write down her license plate number, did you?"

"No, I had no reason to." But now that she thought of it, it would have been a good idea. She had just assumed that her biggest worry was that her sister would try to force her to sell the ranch so Courtney could get her share.

So what had changed?

Zane, she thought as she watched him move the bureau away from the wall. Zane and ten thousand dollars, is that what had changed? If they were right and her birth mother had contacted her, was it possible she'd put Courtney up to this? But why? It made no sense.

No, Dakota thought. This had to have something to do with her and Zane and Courtney being spiteful. But how far was her sister planning to take this? That's what scared her.

She stepped closer to see what Zane was reaching for. "You found something?"

"A credit card receipt. Looks like it was for food and drinks at the bar in Zortman." He held it up. "Is it yours?"

"I can't imagine how it could be. What is the date on it?"

"A week ago."

She shook her head. "I hardly ever get down to Zortman." It was a small old mining town an hour to the south.

"Has anyone else been in this room since then?"

"No. Just Courtney."

He met her gaze. "This could be the bartender who called. He apparently knows more than we do about what Courtney's been up to. How do you feel about hitting that bar down in Zortman? I need to check in at home first. I'm surprised that my brothers don't have the National Guard out looking for me."

"Give me a call when you're ready and I'll drive over to Whitehorse later," Dakota said. "I need to take care of a few things around here first." The lie seemed to hang between them.

"Sure. You know you don't have to go. I can go down and talk to the bartender on my own."

Dakota hesitated, caught between wanting to find Courtney and wanting to put distance between her and Zane and the old feelings he evoked in her.

"No," she said, finding Courtney and her diary winning out. "Just give me a call."

WHEN ZANE'S CELL PHONE RANG, he thought it was Dakota calling to say she'd changed her mind. He'd seen that she hadn't wanted to go with him to Zortman. He didn't blame her. They'd been together now for almost forty-eight hours. Clearly, she'd had enough of him.

He mentally kicked himself for kissing her as he took the call. Had he thought she was still that starry-eyed girl who'd had a crush on him? What had he been thinking?

"Just received those DNA results from the cell phone," Doc said by way of introduction, then paused.

"Yes?"

"Whoever's blood is on the phone, I can tell you that the person is female and related to Dakota Lansing."

"Could it be a sister with the same father, different mothers?" Zane asked.

"Definitely could be from what I see in the DNA report," Doc said.

So Courtney really was her sister. He'd been so sure she wasn't and that she'd been pretending to be Clay Lansing's love child as part of some elaborate scam—a scam that somehow involved him.

And the blood *was* Courtney's. That thought was slow coming, but hit him like a brick. There hadn't been a lot of blood, but enough to scare him.

He had hoped it had been staged and would end up being animal blood.

"You still there?" Doc asked.

"Yeah, sorry, I'm just surprised. Thanks." As he hung up, he turned down his lane and saw the sheriff's SUV sitting in front of his house. He swore under his breath.

He glanced in the rearview mirror and saw his face. It wasn't that much better than it had been yesterday. The scratches were starting to heal, but still shocking.

Worse, he couldn't explain any of it, including the blood on Courtney's phone. Glancing over, he saw the bagged phone sitting on the seat where Dakota had left it. He pocketed the plastic bag with the phone inside and parked next to the SUV, hoping the sheriff wasn't here with bad news.

As he climbed out, he caught a glimpse of McCall's expression and knew whatever she was here for wasn't good.

"Zane," the sheriff said as she climbed awkwardly out of her rig.

He saw the exact moment she got a good look at his face and the scratches. Her expression darkened even more.

"Want to tell me how you got those scratches?" She sounded angry and disappointed.

He was pretty sure she now knew that he'd been hiding in the bathroom the other day so she wouldn't see his face. He swore silently. He looked even more guilty. Worse, the sheriff would know Dakota had been in on it.

"I don't know how I got the scratches," he said honestly. "But I'll tell you what I do know."

She nodded slowly. "Maybe we better step inside your house. You have a problem with that?"

He shook his head. He knew he should probably call the ranch lawyer. At the very least make her get a warrant. But he feared that would only make matters worse. He knew McCall, knew the kind of sheriff she was. All he could do was put his cards on the table.

Once inside the house, he offered the sheriff a seat as well as something to drink. Not surprisingly, she wasn't in the mood for either.

He told her everything, leaving out nothing but making sure he covered for Dakota.

When he finished, McCall said, "Where is this suitcase with the money in it?"

"It's in my truck behind the seat."

"Let's go get it," the sheriff said.

While he dug out the suitcase, she stood behind him.

"If you don't mind, you can put it in my car," she said, opening the passenger side door of the SUV for him to load the suitcase. "Then I'd like to have a look around your house. With your permission."

"Fine with me," he said as he led her back to the house. As they entered, he told her, "There's a broken lamp on the other side of the bed. I have no idea how it got broken."

"And the cell phone you found under the bed?" she asked.

Reluctantly, he produced it from his pocket.

She raised a brow when she saw that he'd placed it in a sandwich bag—and that it had what she must recognize as blood on it.

"The blood belongs to Courtney Baxter, although that's not her legal name, according to her mother. It's Courtney Hughes."

The sheriff didn't seem surprised at that news. "You should have come to me right away."

"I knew even less then than I do now. I wanted to find Courtney first."

McCall looked around the small house, going into the bedroom last. The covers on the bed were still rumpled; everything looked as it had when he'd awakened from what he now thought of as his mystery date from hell.

He watched McCall awkwardly bend down to look under the bed, saw her freeze and felt his heart drop. What of interest could possibly be under the bed? There'd been nothing under there when he'd found the phone.

She rose long enough to pull on latex gloves, then bent down again to pull out a red dress—the dress Courtney Baxter had been wearing when she'd appeared at his door two nights before.

Even from the bedroom doorway, he saw the dark stains on the silken fabric. More blood.

"That wasn't under the bed when I left here yesterday," he said, his denial sounding hollow, his voice tight with dread. "I'm being set up. I swear to you...."

McCall pushed herself to her feet and turned to face him. The rest of his words died off as he saw her expression.

"Zane Chisholm. You have the right to remain silent," she began as she bagged the dress, then reached for her handcuffs.

Chapter Eight

Emma looked forward to trips into Whitehorse even though Mrs. Crowley was far from a fun companion. She spoke little and became irritated quickly if Emma tried to force conversation.

But being a recluse, Mrs. Crowley made it easy for Emma to have some free time away from everyone. It was their secret that Mrs. Crowley dropped her off to do her errands and picked her up hours later. For that Emma was eternally grateful.

Hoyt would have a fit if he knew. But Emma felt safe in Whitehorse. She still carried a pistol in her purse and kept on the lookout for anyone who didn't seem familiar.

It hadn't taken long to tell the locals from the occasional tourist passing through town. Whitehorse didn't get a lot of tourists. Most people came to Montana to see the mountains, towering pine trees and clear, fast streams. They had little interest in the rolling prairie, which was short on mountains, pines and streams.

Today though, Emma found herself wondering where Mrs. Crowley spent those free hours. The housekeeper never complained. In fact, she seemed to enjoy the time alone. Or maybe she just enjoyed being shed of Emma after the twenty-mile trip into town.

Emma knew she talked too much. But after being around so many men at the ranch, she was thankful to find herself in a woman's company—even Mrs. Crowley. She was excited at the idea of spending some hours on her own. The past year had been difficult. She had always been extremely independent. Being tied down and required to always have someone with her had been hell for her.

Not that she ever regretted marrying Hoyt. That was why she tried hard not to complain. This wasn't his fault, and she didn't want him blaming himself.

Today she had thoroughly enjoyed herself in town and was almost sorry when Mrs. Crowley pulled up in the truck for the ride home.

As she climbed into the passenger side, she noticed that Mrs. Crowley looked disheveled, which was completely out of character. Also the cab of the pickup smelled odd. She glanced more closely at the woman behind the wheel.

"Is something wrong?" she asked, taking in the death grip the housekeeper had on the steering wheel.

"I'm fine," Mrs. Crowley snapped.

Emma bit her tongue; however, she couldn't help noticing that there was dirt under the woman's fingernails. How odd.

It wasn't until she got out of the truck at the ranch that she saw the shovel in the pickup bed. It was covered with dark soil.

ZANE THOUGHT ABOUT USING his one phone call to contact the ranch lawyer. Instead, he called Dakota.

"I've been arrested," he said the moment she answered her cell. "When I got back to the house, the sheriff was waiting for me. She found something under the bed that wasn't there yesterday."

"What was it?" Dakota asked, sounding scared.

"It was the dress Courtney was wearing the night she showed up at my door. Dakota, it looks like there is blood on it."

"Oh, Zane. You're sure the dress wasn't under the bed when you found the phone?"

"Positive." He never locked his house. Hardly anyone around Whitehorse did. But he mentally kicked himself for not thinking to do it yesterday when they'd left. He had made it too easy for whoever was trying to frame him. He'd thought the damage was already done. He'd been wrong about that.

"Someone is definitely setting me up. I'm just scared that something has happened to Courtney. Could you call my dad? I used my one call to phone you."

"Of course. And I'll follow up on that receipt we found behind the bureau."

"No, don't. Please. It's too dangerous. Whoever is behind this…I'm afraid they're playing for keeps."

"You think Courtney is dead." Her voice broke and he could hear how scared she was that it was true.

"I hate to be the one to tell you this, but I heard as I was being led into the sheriff's department that Courtney's car was found in a ravine south of town. That was apparently why the sheriff was waiting at my house. I think McCall found more evidence against me in the car." He hesitated. "There's something else, Dakota. Doc called me. The DNA test results? Courtney *is* your sister."

DAKOTA HUNG UP, SHAKEN by the news. Zane in jail on possible murder charges. Courtney *was* her half sister— just as she'd claimed. And now she might be dead, her car in a ravine and more evidence against Zane in it?

She felt a sense of panic mixed with worry and heartfelt pain. She hadn't trusted Courtney. Still didn't. All she could hope was that her sister was alive and behind some scheme to make it appear Zane had done her harm.

It still made no sense. Courtney wouldn't take sibling rivalry this far. There had to be more to this.

Dakota reminded herself that her sister wasn't working alone. Who was this other person? Her birth mother?

She shuddered at the thought of Courtney's bloody dress being found under Zane's bed. Whoever was setting him up was building a strong case against him.

Dakota hurriedly called the Chisholm ranch, anxious to let Emma and Hoyt know what was going on so they could get Zane a good lawyer.

A woman answered the phone, her voice a little gravelly. "Chisholm Ranch, Mrs. Crowley speaking."

Mrs. Crowley? Zane hadn't mentioned anyone by that name. "I'm calling for Hoyt Chisholm."

"I'm sorry, he isn't in. May I take a message?"

Dakota heard someone ask, "Who is it?" then "I'll take it, Mrs. Crowley."

"Hello? This is Emma Chisholm, can I help you?"

Dakota introduced herself and quickly told her what had happened. "I'm sorry to have to tell you this over the phone."

"No, I appreciate you calling for Zane. It's just that... I'm shocked," Emma said.

"I'm sure Zane will fill you in on everything that's happened. You'll make sure his lawyer is called?"

"Of course. Thank you for letting me know."

Dakota hung up, unable to shake her fear for Zane—and Courtney. The way this was escalating, she couldn't believe Courtney had known what she was getting into.

As she glanced around the empty ranch house, she realized that she was spooked. She'd never been scared living out here so far from any other houses. The ranch had always been a safe place.

Until Courtney showed up, she thought with a shiver.

Zane had told her not to drive to Zortman and talk to the bartender, but when she considered all the evidence stacking up against him, she knew she couldn't just sit back and do nothing.

She didn't believe for an instant that Zane would hurt Courtney. It scared her though. If Courtney's car had been found and there was even more incriminating evidence in it... Was Courtney still alive? She shuddered at the thought that it might be too late for the sister she hadn't even gotten to know. Ultimately, blood was thicker than water. Whoever was behind this was going to pay.

Dakota reached for her purse. Maybe she couldn't save her sister; maybe no one could. But she would move heaven and hell to prove that Zane was innocent of this. She'd never been to the Miner's Bar in Zortman, but she'd heard stories about how rough it was when the gold mine had been up and running.

Still, she knew it would be at least a while before the ranch attorney could get Zane before a judge, and there was always the chance he wouldn't be able to make bail.

Dakota feared that whoever was behind this would

be tying up any loose ends. If Courtney was still alive, then Dakota had to move quickly. She felt as if the clock was ticking, the noose around Zane's neck tightening as well.

As she headed for her pickup, Dakota tried to imagine why Courtney would agree to be part of this. Ten thousand dollars? There had to be more to it. Courtney had grown up in a nice house with two parents who loved her and provided well for her. Also, Courtney hadn't thought enough about the money to put it somewhere safer than under the bed—or take it with her.

It had to be something more alluring than cash.

Courtney's birth mother. With a start, Dakota realized what a pull that could have had on her sister. Courtney was an only child who had never known her father or mother.

Dakota knew what it was like not having a mother. What had it been like for Courtney not knowing either of her birth parents? Maybe she had yearned for that connection, someone who she resembled, more than her adopted mother had known.

Family. Was that the hook that had gotten Courtney involved in what she might have thought at first was innocent?

Clearly she hadn't realized how dangerous it was. Now, if Courtney was still alive, she would definitely be a loose end.

DAKOTA CALLED MINER'S BAR on her way to Zortman. She figured that even if the bartender wasn't working, he wouldn't be that hard to find.

Zortman was a small, old mining town, even smaller

than Whitehorse. It squatted at the edge of the Little Rockies, surrounded by pine trees and rock cliffs.

"He ain't here," said a male voice as if this was his standard, humorous response when answering the phone. Dakota could hear chuckling in the background. It was an old bar joke, the typical line when a woman called.

She recognized the man's voice at once. It was the same man who'd answered the number on Courtney's cell phone earlier.

He laughed a little too long at his own joke. "Sorry, Miner's Bar. What can I do you for?" More chuckles.

Apparently the crowd was eating it up or was drunk enough to laugh at anything. Dakota figured it was probably the latter since it was late afternoon.

"Hello?" he said, his voice becoming muffled as if he'd turned away from the crowd at the bar. "Anyone there?" His tone changed. "Court?" he asked in a whisper.

Dakota snapped the cell phone shut and looked down the long straight road toward the Little Rockies. She didn't mind the drive south. This time of year the rolling prairie was lush and green, the sky a crystal clear, blinding blue. Only a few large white cumulus clouds hung on the horizon ahead.

A hawk called to her from a fence post as she passed. She'd just seen a bald eagle near a group of antelope. The antelope had spooked. She'd watched them race to the nearest barbed wire fence, scurry under it and take off again, disappearing over a rise. The eagle still hadn't moved, she saw in her rearview mirror.

As she drove through the ponderosas into Zortman, she spotted Miner's Bar among the other log buildings.

It appeared old, the logs weathered. She parked, got out, breathed in the scent of pines and went over again how she was going to play this.

She was Courtney's sister. That much wasn't a lie. Dakota was betting that if the bartender knew about the people her sister had gotten involved with, then the sister wouldn't come as a surprise.

Pushing open the door, Dakota was hit with the smell of stale beer. The bar was like so many in this part of Montana. Small and dark, a bunch of regulars on stools along the bar, a sad Western song playing on the jukebox.

And like bars in out-of-the-way places in Montana, everyone turned as she came in. She felt their gazes as the door shut behind her. Only a few were still staring at her as she made her way to an empty stool at the far end of the bar.

Once people didn't recognize you, they usually went back to their drinking. Only a couple of the younger cowboys at the bar leered at her longer.

"Go get her, Wyatt," one of them said, loud enough for her to hear, as the bartender stopped what he was doing to head in her direction. The others at the bar laughed. Clearly they'd had a few drinks and were looking for some fun.

Dakota studied the bartender as he made his way down the bar. Wyatt was tall, broad-shouldered and not bad looking. There was stubble on his jaw. His blond hair was rumpled and he had a look in his blue eyes that she recognized. She would bet he was exactly Courtney's type.

"What'll you have?" he asked, giving her a grin. She'd also bet someone had told him his grin was irresistible to women. It wouldn't be the first time the man had been lied to, or the last.

She could feel the group down the bar watching now. They'd probably been watching him in action for as long as he'd worked here.

"Whatever you have on tap," she told him.

Wyatt raised a brow. "Gotta love a woman who drinks beer," he said, flirting with her as he poured her one from the tap nearby.

"Does my sister drink beer?" Dakota asked quietly as he set down a bar napkin and her glass of beer.

He leaned toward her as if he wasn't sure he'd heard her. "Your sister?"

"Courtney," she said, still keeping her voice down.

He froze, then picked up a rag and killed some time wiping down the scarred surface of the bar. She could tell he was sizing her up, figuring out what to say, afraid he'd mess up.

"I know she spent some time here. With you." She met his gaze. She figured those nights Courtney had come in late she'd been down here. From Wyatt's expression, she'd figured right.

Wyatt put down the rag, wiped a hand over his mouth and asked, "She told you about me?"

"I'm her sister."

He seemed to relax, even let out a small laugh. "The uptight daddy's cowgirl."

The uptight daddy's cowgirl? So that was how Courtney had described her. Maybe her theory about the sibling rivalry wasn't that far off. Courtney *had* resented the fact that Dakota had had their father all those years and she hadn't. She bristled at the "uptight" part, though.

"And you're her latest sucker," Dakota said to Wyatt, and took a long drink of her beer.

He frowned, angry now. "Hey, watch it. I'm no sucker," he said in a tight whisper.

Dakota lifted a brow as she put down her beer. It was cold and tasted good. She wiped the foam from her upper lip. "So you're saying she didn't stick you with her bar bill?"

He leaned against the bar. "Are you trying to tell me she won't be back? Is that what this is about? She sent you with a message for me? Or didn't she get the money?"

"She got the money, but she seems to have disappeared. Actually, I'm looking for her myself."

He laughed. "She owes you money, too, huh?"

"She's part con artist, no doubt about that. But I'm afraid we're both going to be out of luck if I don't find her. I don't like the people she's…involved with."

"Yeah, me either."

Dakota took another drink of her beer. She had to go slow. If she rushed this, he might spook. But if she gave him too much time to think…

"Of course, she could be lying to both of us."

Wyatt shook his head. "Not if she already got the money. It must just be taking her longer than she thought it would."

So Courtney *had* been paid to do something. Dakota was dying to ask him if he knew what she had to do for the ten thousand dollars. "You think the money is why she's doing this?" Dakota let out a disbelieving sound and took another drink.

"Why else?"

She shrugged. "I think her birth mother has her hooks in her." She took a chance, winging it.

He looked surprised. "She told you about her?"

Dakota didn't bother to answer. "Courtney was worried she couldn't trust the woman. What do you think?"

She could see that he liked being asked what he thought. He even gave it a few seconds of thought before he spoke.

"I think family's what it's all about. Court got choked up even talking about her. It's her *blood,* you know what I mean?"

"Yeah. I get that." She held his gaze.

"Sure, you're her sister. So you're going to do right by her." The last came out almost sounding like a question. Courtney must have told him about the ranch and the business. She'd been eyeing it along with whatever else she was up to, just as Dakota had suspected.

"Still, I'd like to meet her mother, make sure she's on the up-and-up."

"Yeah, me too, but Court wasn't havin' it. I said, 'bring her down to the bar,' but she said her mother doesn't get out much." He shrugged.

"But if the mother's staying in Whitehorse…"

"Up north near the border, I think. Court never really said. I just got the feeling she wasn't in town."

"She mention what her mother wanted her to do for this money?"

He looked wary. "Nope." He didn't ask if Courtney had told her. Clearly, he knew Courtney had no intention of telling *her.* Did that mean he knew her old connection to Zane Chisholm?

Dakota tried a different tactic, seeing that she was losing him. "I would have thought she'd have told you how she had to earn this money her mother was giving her."

He smiled, proving he wasn't as stupid as he appeared. "I should get back down the bar."

"I know Courtney was worried. She took one of our father's pistols."

Wyatt tried to hide his surprise but failed. He held up both hands. "I don't know anything about it." One of the regulars called to him for another drink. He took a step in that direction.

Dakota put a twenty on the bar along with one of her father's business cards with the house's landline number on it. "My name's Dakota Lansing. If you hear from Courtney " He started to argue. "She's already called me once saying she was in trouble and needed help. Unfortunately, the line went dead right after that."

He looked scared now. Another regular hollered at him, told him to quit flirting and bring them something to drink, but he didn't move. "I had a bad feeling about this. But I swear, she didn't tell me what she had to do for her mother. Just that she had to do it. She swore it was no big deal. Kind of a prank, really."

A prank? Dakota watched him hightail it down the bar. His hands were shaking as he reached for a couple of bottles of beer in the cooler. He'd suspected it was more than that. Who got paid ten thousand dollars by their mother to be part of a prank?

Wyatt had to know at least a little of what Courtney had been up to, Dakota thought as she left the twenty and her father's business card and walked out of the bar.

"Guess you didn't get far with that one," one of the regulars said, and they all laughed as the door closed behind her.

THE STATE CRIME TECHS FOUND the body buried under about six inches of dirt, fifty yards away from where Courtney Baxter's lime-green car was discovered.

McCall got the call late in the afternoon and drove south to the ravine. Coroner George Murphy was already on the scene.

"What have we got?" she asked after trudging through the cactus and sagebrush to the shallow grave. All the crime tech had told her on the phone was that they'd found a body in a shallow grave near where the car had gone off the road.

"The body was dumped here and hastily covered with dirt." George looked a little green around the gills. McCall knew the feeling. She never got used to violent death. It had gotten worse with pregnancy.

"Time of death?"

"I would estimate sometime in the past twenty-four hours. It appears the body was either thrown or rolled off that bluff," George said, pointing to a spot up by the road.

"It wasn't carried?"

He shook his head.

"So the killer might not have been very strong," McCall noted. "Could be why the body wasn't buried more deeply."

"Could be," he agreed. "I suppose you want to see the body." He didn't wait for an answer. He simply unzipped the black bag and stepped back.

McCall let out a surprised, "Who's that?" She'd expected to see Courtney Baxter.

"Your guess is as good as mine," George said. "He didn't have any identification on him. The crime techs took his fingerprints. He has what looks like prison tattoos, so they're pretty sure they'll get an ID on him as soon as they run his prints."

The man, short and slightly built, had been hit in the face with a flat, blunt object; his features were no longer recognizable. Blood was matted in his thinning, dark hair, his fingernails were dirty and broken, his clothing soiled from spending at least twenty-four hours under a pile of dirt.

McCall leaned away from the body, motioning for George to zip the bag up again. Her stomach lurched and she had to turn away from the smell not to be sick.

George handed her a mint. She mumbled her thanks and gazed up at the road, then over to the junipers where Courtney Baxter's car had been found.

"The crime team is broadening its search," George said. "They seem to think there might be another grave out here."

"Courtney Baxter's," McCall said, glad her stomach was finally settling down. "Unless Courtney's the killer."

"McCall, you are the most suspicious person I know," George said as he came over to stand by her. In the distance, crime scene techs were using cadaver dogs to search for more bodies. "I hope I never get like you."

"You will. If you stay at this long enough," she said.

ZANE DIALED DAKOTA'S CELL phone number the moment he made bail. One of the benefits of being a Chisholm was that his father was a powerful rancher and had pull when it came to the local judge. Thanks to his father, he wasn't going to have to spend even one night in jail. At least not yet.

Hoyt Chisholm and the ranch lawyer had convinced

the judge that Zane wasn't a flight risk. So far, all the sheriff had was incriminating evidence, but no body.

Zane knew that if Courtney was found dead it could change everything. He didn't even want to think about that. Whoever was behind this was bound to hear he'd made bail. He didn't doubt they would step up their plan to frame him.

As he listened to Dakota's phone go to voice mail, he knew he was waiting for the other shoe to drop.

He had to find out who was behind this before any more "evidence" appeared. His brother Marshall had dropped off his pickup when he'd come in with their father for the bail hearing. He started the engine as he listened to Dakota's voice mail message. Where was she?

He left a message saying he was out on bail and had to see her. He couldn't help being worried about her and didn't like the idea of her staying at the Lansing ranch by herself.

After a moment, he tried the number again. This time when it went to voice mail, he left a message saying he was headed for her ranch and for her to sit tight. He had to see her.

He knew his father and brothers, along with Emma, were anxious to see him. They wanted an explanation. He wished he had one to give them.

But he was too worried about Dakota to do that right now. Worse, he feared she might have decided to do some investigating on her own. She'd mentioned going down to Zortman to talk to the bartender. He'd told her not to go. Unfortunately, he feared that might have been like waving a red flag in front of a bull.

He quickly placed a call home. "I have to make a

stop before I come there," Zane told his father when he answered.

"Zane—"

"I'll be there as soon as I can. This is important. Would you ask Emma to make sure one of the guest rooms is ready? I'll be bringing a friend with me." He hung up before his father could question him further.

The hard part would be convincing Dakota to come back to the Chisholm ranch with him. The woman was independent, which he liked. But the more he'd thought about everything while in jail, the more he feared she was in danger.

Chapter Nine

It was late by the time Dakota left Zortman. Clouds scudded across a black velvet sky, giving her only fleeting glimpses of a sliver of silver moon.

Exhausted after a long, emotionally draining day, she drove back to the ranch. She was anxious to talk to Zane so she could tell him what she'd found out. She hadn't been able to get any service while on her way to Miner's Bar or on the way back until she reached Chinook.

She checked her messages. Both from Zane. He was out on bail and was headed for her ranch? She half expected to see his pickup when she pulled into the yard. *He must be on his way,* she thought as she climbed out and went inside.

It had been a long day. She wondered if she had time for a hot bath before Zane arrived. She was anxious to talk to him, even more anxious to see him.

Dakota sensed something was wrong the moment she walked into her father's ranch house. She hit the light switch and nothing happened. For just an instant, she thought the bulb in the overhead light had simply burned out.

Then she smelled him.

The hair shot up on the back of her neck. Goose bumps skittered over her flesh as she started to turn, her mouth opening as she tried to find her voice.

Her throat contracted and before she could squeeze out a sound, he was on her. His large hand clamped over her mouth, his arm wrapping around her, snatching her back against him in a viselike grip.

She kicked, tried to free her arms to fight him, but he was so much larger, so much stronger, that she was pinned. He dragged her toward the back of the house, knocking over a chair, then a lamp. The lamp broke, sounding like a shot, as he carried her away in the darkness.

Dakota heard a vehicle coming up the road. She tried to scream, but he had his hand over her mouth and his arm around her, pinning her own arms at her sides.

He shoved her through the open side door of a dark-colored van. She tried to scramble away from him. He caught her leg, dragged her to him and then hit her with his fist.

Stars glittered before her eyes just before the darkness closed in.

"DAKOTA?" ZANE KNOCKED, then tried her door. It swung open. He glanced back at her pickup parked outside. After he'd parked, he'd walked by her truck, felt heat still coming off the engine. She couldn't have been home long.

His fear was that she'd gone down to Miner's Bar in Zortman and put herself in even more danger. "Dakota?"

It was pitch-black inside the house. He tried the light switch. Nothing. Only a faint sliver of moon lit the sky outside, but was quickly extinguished by the cover of clouds. It did little to illuminate the interior of the house even though the curtains were all open. Out here in the middle of nowhere, curtains were seldom closed. No point.

"Dakota?" he called louder as his pulse took off.

The modest ranch house was single-level, the layout allowing him to move swiftly through it. "Dakota?" He heard the growing fear in his voice. Then, in a sudden shaft of moonlight he saw the upended chair and shattered lamp scattered across the floor, and felt the cool breeze coming through the open back door.

He raced to the door, his heart in his throat. In the distance, he heard a vehicle engine turn over. Swearing, he rushed outside into the darkness. He cleared the edge of the yard in time to see a van roar down the road.

Zane tore around the side of the house to his truck, leaped behind the wheel and cranked the engine over. He hadn't gone far when he felt the pickup lean to the right and heard the *whap whap* of the back rear tire.

Even before he stopped and got out he knew what he was going to find. Someone had cut his tire.

He stared after the taillights of the van as they dimmed on the horizon, his heart pounding with fear. Someone had Dakota. One sister was already missing. Now Dakota.

Call the sheriff.

As he reached for his phone, it rang.

"We have Dakota," a deep male voice said.

Zane had to tamp down his relief. He'd been expecting a call about Courtney and that one had never come. He'd feared the same might be true of Dakota.

"Who's *we?*" he asked, not expecting an answer but needing to fill the silence.

"If you ever want to see her again, you will do exactly as I say. Call the sheriff and I kill her."

"I won't. But don't you hurt her."

A hoarse chuckle. "Then you do what I say." He proceeded to give directions to an old mission cemetery outside of Whitehorse. "You know the place?"

"Yes." The mission building had been boarded up for years and the cemetery was surrounded by an iron fence. Both sat on a hill in the middle of nowhere. The perfect place for an ambush, especially on such a dark night.

"Twenty minutes? Bring the money."

"I'll be there."

"Come alone."

"Of course."

"And unarmed. You'd better get that tire fixed and get movin'. Time is running out for this cowgirl."

"I'm not movin' until I know that Dakota is all right."

The man started to argue, then swore. Zane could hear the scrape of his boot soles on the ground, then the groan of the rusty van door as he opened it.

A moment later, he heard what sounded like duct tape being ripped from her mouth. Dakota gave out a small cry.

"Tell him you're fine," the man ordered.

"Zane, don't—"

Another cry from Dakota, what sounded like a struggle, then the man's deep voice again. "Happy? She's fine as long as you do what I say."

Zane's free hand balled up in a fist. He couldn't wait to get his hands on the bastard. He hung up and dug out the .38 pistol he kept under his pickup seat, making sure it was loaded.

Then he stuffed the weapon into the pocket of his jean jacket and slipped his hunting knife in its scabbard into the top of his boot.

Twelve minutes later, he'd changed his pickup tire and was headed in the direction of the old mission. He didn't have the money. The sheriff had confiscated it. Apparently whoever had taken Dakota didn't know that.

So that would change how things went down, he thought, as ahead he saw the old mission etched against the dark sky.

MRS. CROWLEY HEARD the commotion shortly after the ranch phone rang. She glanced at her clock. Something was going on, since it was late in the evening. She'd been in bed, but not asleep, her drapes closed, making her room dark as the inside of a coffin.

Easing out of bed, she made her way to the door. Her room was in an empty wing away from the rest of the house. That was a blessing—and a disadvantage. She had to leave her room and sneak down the hallway to the stairs to hear anything that was going on.

Getting caught was not an option. But she was more than a little curious. She crept down the hallway to the top of the stairs, then settled herself into the deep shadows to listen.

"That's all he said?" Emma's insistent voice was followed by Hoyt's low rumble.

"I just know he was arrested because some woman he went out with is missing. He promised to come out here and tell me what's going on. But as you can see, he isn't here."

"Why would he want a guest room ready unless he was bringing someone with him?" Emma had dropped her voice. They were both on the lower wing where the guest rooms were located.

"I have no idea. Believe me, I'd like to know what the hell is going on as much as you do. I'm worried that something else has happened."

"Should we call the sheriff?" Emma asked.

"No. We'll wait and hope for the best."

Mrs. Crowley heard them go toward the kitchen. She knew Emma would make a pot of coffee, then probably bake something. The woman couldn't quit baking.

Sighing, she sneaked back to her room. Normally she never looked out her window, and kept the drapes shut tightly. But now she opened them a crack and peered out.

A breeze stirred the tall, old cottonwoods next to the house. Through the leafy limbs, she caught glimpses of moon and starlight. A dark night. Her favorite. She opened the window a crack and breathed in the air even though it tasted bitter to her, the scent too familiar, too painful.

She closed the window quietly and climbed back into bed. She knew she wasn't going to be able to sleep. As she lay staring up at the ceiling, she smiled to herself. Apparently there was trouble in Chisholm ranch paradise. There would be no lovemaking tonight in that king-size bed on the second floor of the other wing, or out in the barn.

Mrs. Crowley rubbed a hand over her smooth face. She would be glad when she no longer had to pretend to be someone she wasn't. And that time was coming. Soon.

Zane slowed at the turnoff into the old mission. His headlights caught on a dark-colored van parked in the shadow of the church. It sat at an odd angle, the side door open. As the headlights hit it, Zane saw that the van was empty.

As he drove in, his headlights slashed over the terra-cotta-colored stucco of the church structure, then picked up the bone-white of some of the gravestones higher up the hill.

He parked next to the van, killed his lights and engine and sat for a moment, listening with his side window down.

Clouds played peekaboo with the crescent moon and sky full of stars, keeping the night dark with floating shadows across the landscape. An owl hooted from its perch on the ridge of the church roof. Back on the highway, a semi roared past. Silence followed.

Zane eased his door open and, grabbing an old duffel bag from behind the seat of his pickup, stepped out. The bag had a couple pairs of his old leather branding gloves in it. Ten thousand dollars in hundred dollar bills didn't take up a lot of space. He figured it would be enough weight to fool the kidnapper since Zane had no intention of ever letting the man look inside the bag.

The kidnapper couldn't be inside the church, since it had been boarded up for years. That didn't leave many hiding places.

Moving slowly, Zane climbed the slope toward the graveyard. At the edge of the building he stopped to make sure the kidnapper wasn't hiding in the shadow of the church.

The moon came out from behind a cloud, painting the side of the church in silver. No sign of anyone next to the church, but they could have moved around to the highway side.

He had his doubts about that. A man holding a woman at gunpoint could be seen in the glare of lights from the highway. Zane doubted the man would take that chance.

Turning his gaze back to the graveyard, he continued up the hillside. There could be only one other place the kidnapper was hiding with Dakota.

Most of the gravestones were too small and narrow to hide behind. But as he climbed higher, he saw several larger tombstones, these closer together and deeper in shadow.

"I'm here," he called as he moved toward the larger moss-covered gravestones.

Something moved in the dark twenty yards in front of him. He could make out the man's huge shape against the black sky and see the man's arm locked around Dakota's neck. As he moved closer, he caught the faint glint of a gun; the barrel was next to her head.

"Keep your hands where I can see them," the man called out. "Did you bring the money?"

Zane held the bag out away from his body as he moved toward the man, keeping his gaze on Dakota. She had a strip of duct tape over her mouth and her hands were bound behind her.

As Zane approached slowly, the moon and a few stars broke free of the clouds, casting an eerie, ghost-like glow over the graveyard. He locked eyes on Dakota and saw the determined gleam burning there. The man hadn't hurt her, but he had made her furious.

He smiled to himself in relief. Even after the years apart, he knew this woman. From the look on her face, she was ready for whatever he had in mind. With the relief came a surge of love. Dakota had always been strong. He needed her to be strong now as he prayed that he didn't get her killed.

When he passed one of the taller headstones, he pretended to stumble on the uneven ground and surreptitiously dropped his gun behind the gravestone before taking a few more steps toward the kidnapper.

"That's close enough," the man said.

Stopping ten feet away from the man, Zane set down the duffel bag and took a step back from it. "Now let her go."

The man shook his head. "Not until you hand over the money. Throw it to me."

Zane took another step back, now within feet of the tombstone where he'd dropped his weapon. "We had a deal. I brought your money. Let her go."

He could see the man's indecision even in the dark. He wanted the money badly. He was nervous and afraid; clearly this wasn't something he did every day.

Zane watched as the man took a step toward the bag, dragging Dakota with him. She was making it as difficult as possible for him to keep the gun on her and move her forward.

The man swore and released her, giving her a push that sent her sprawling between two old, bleached-white gravestones.

The moment she hit the ground, she disappeared into the darkness. Zane heard her scramble away from the man.

The kidnapper swore and hurried to the bag as Zane backed up to the gravestone where he'd dropped his pistol.

As the man reached for the bag, Zane reached for his gun. Slipping behind the tombstone, he raised it to aim at the kidnapper's chest.

The man, intent on the money, didn't seem to notice at first that Zane had suddenly dropped down behind a gravestone ten feet away.

But when he did, he brought his gun up and got off a shot. The bullet ricocheted off the crumbling stone inches from Zane's head. The man started to dodge toward one of the headstones for cover. But even moving, he made a large target. The first bullet didn't seem to faze him.

Zane fired again, dropping the man to his knees. He'd dropped the bag a few feet from him. He made a move for it. Zane fired into the dirt next to the duffel bag and the man jerked his hand back.

"Where is Courtney Baxter?" he called to the kidnapper. "What have you done with her?"

The kidnapper looked up, surprised by the question. "You're asking the wrong person," he called back as he made another lunge for the bag.

Zane's next bullet caught the big man in the leg.

He let out a howl, stumbled awkwardly to his feet again and charged, getting off two shots that pelted the gravestone around Zane and sent rock chips into the air.

Zane fired once more, the man just feet from him. The final shot stopped the kidnapper cold. He stood like a lumbering pine swaying in the wind before toppling, coming down with a crash that stirred the dust around him.

Zane kicked the man's gun away from him and then knelt down to check for a pulse. He found none. The air smelled of gunpowder, the night suddenly deathly quiet again.

"Dakota," Zane called as he got to his feet.

She stumbled out of the deep shadows of the gravestones. She had managed to cut the tape around her wrists on something she'd found in the cemetery and was freeing her hands as she came out of the dark.

He took her in his arms. "Did he hurt you?"

She shook her head, removed the tape from her mouth and pressed her face into his chest.

"Did you recognize him?" he asked.

"I'd never seen him before."

With one arm holding Dakota, Zane pulled out his cell and was surprised to get service this far from a town. He punched in 911.

EMMA TALKED HOYT INTO GOING to bed after Zane called to say something had come up. "He said he would see us in the morning. Whatever is going on, apparently it is going to have to wait until morning."

Hoyt tried Zane's number. It went straight to voice mail. He finally went to bed and instantly fell to sleep.

Emma felt as if she'd just closed her eyes when she heard a vehicle. She checked the clock and was surprised to see that she'd slept for hours. It was almost three in the morning.

She went to the window, expecting to see Zane and whoever he'd wanted the guest room for.

"Mrs. Crowley?" What could the woman possibly be doing out this late on these nights?

Even as she told herself it was none of her business, she watched Mrs. Crowley slip into the house. For a long moment Emma eyed the pickup the woman used.

Finally, knowing she wasn't going to get any sleep if she didn't, she pulled on Hoyt's dark robe and sneaked downstairs.

At the bottom, she stopped to listen. Not a sound came from Mrs. Crowley's wing of the house. Still, she waited. She would have a hard time pretending she'd merely come downstairs for a glass of water if Mrs. Crowley caught her.

Of course, there was always sleepwalking. Emma shoved that thought away with a snort. Mrs. Crowley would see right through that. The woman had an uncanny ability when it came to reading people.

Still not a sound.

In the kitchen, she slid open the utility drawer and felt around until her fingers closed on the small flashlight Hoyt kept there.

She ran the beam over the extra keys on the peg by the door until she found the spare key for the pickup Mrs. Crowley had been given to use.

Then she quickly turned off the flashlight and stood, gripping the key and listening.

She hated sneaking around her own house. But she knew that thought had more to do with her own guilty conscience, given what she was planning to do.

Snugging Hoyt's robe around her small frame, she tiptoed through the living room to the front door. The house was never locked—until Aggie Wells had come into their lives with stories about Hoyt's first wife coming back from the dead.

Emma eased the door open slowly. It creaked and her heart stopped. She listened, then slipped out onto the porch. The night air felt good. She breathed it in, studying the horizon.

She never got tired of the view of rolling grasslands, the Little Rockies in the distance, a dark purple smudge in the starlight. Emma loved the smell of fresh earth and new, green grasses. She loved Montana and Hoyt, she thought as her heart gave a small kick.

What was she doing spying on their housekeeper?

She almost changed her mind and went back inside. But then she noticed the muddy tires of the pickup they'd given Mrs. Crowley to drive.

There hadn't been any rain this far north, but she'd heard a storm had blown through down in the Missouri Breaks.

Maybe Mrs. Crowley had gone sightseeing.

Until three in the morning?

The air suddenly felt cold. She pulled the robe tighter and made her way quietly to the pickup, keeping to the shadows of the house.

Mrs. Crowley's room was on the far side of the wing, but she had access to every room in the house.

Emma glanced up. All the curtains on this side were open, the glass dark behind them. Fortunately Mrs. Crowley always parked the truck at the end of the wing in the darkest part of the yard.

Emma quickly slipped around the side of the pickup farthest from the house and eased open the passenger side door.

The dome light came on. She quickly turned it off. Then, leaving the door open, she slid across the seat and behind the wheel.

She didn't want to turn on the flashlight, so she felt around until she found the ignition. She slipped the key in after a few awkward attempts and turned it.

When she heard it click, she pulled the tiny flashlight

from the robe pocket and, shielding it with her hand, shone the light on the dashboard.

After quickly memorizing the mileage, she turned off the light, removed the key and slipped back out of the pickup.

As she started to ease the passenger side door shut, she caught a smell that made her stomach roil. It smelled like something had died in the cab of the truck. She thought about the shovel caked with fresh soil and the dirt under Mrs. Crowley's fingernails after the last trip to town and shuddered.

The pickup door clicked shut. She pushed to make sure it had latched and then sneaked back along the house. When she reached the porch, she took one of the chairs and sat for a moment, her heart pounding.

I'm too old for this.

The thought made her chuckle to herself. She would never be too old for this. A sense of satisfaction filled her. She was going to find out what Mrs. Crowley was up to at night, if for no other reason than her own curiosity.

The woman had way too many secrets.

Chapter Ten

"Oh dear, what happened to the two of you?" Emma cried as she ushered Zane and Dakota into the house.

Dakota knew they both looked a mess after what they'd been through last night. They were both dirty and exhausted, Zane's scratches still prominent.

They'd spent the rest of the night at the sheriff's department answering questions and being grilled about the dead man. Zane had been anxious to get to the ranch, so they hadn't even eaten since yesterday at noon.

Hoyt stepped up to his son, reached for his hand and then pulled him into a quick hug. Dakota saw the fear in the older man's face and knew how relieved he must be. Her own father would have felt the same way. She thought of him and felt her eyes blur with tears.

"What you must have been through," Emma said to Dakota. Dakota shuddered as she remembered being taken captive last night. "Oh, sweetheart, it's all right."

Zane put an arm around her and pulled her close.

"The sheriff called and told us some of it," Hoyt said. "But I'd like to hear it from you."

Zane nodded. "This is Dakota Lansing."

Hoyt Chisholm's eyes widened in surprise. "Clay's girl. I was sorry to hear about your father."

She nodded numbly, and Emma ushered them into the kitchen where she served them hot coffee and cranberry coffee cake. Dakota ate two pieces; the cake was the best she'd ever eaten.

"Can I fix you breakfast?" Emma asked, no doubt seeing how Dakota had scarfed down the coffee cake.

"Not now," Hoyt said, and waved a hand at her. Then he quickly smiled over at her. "I'm sorry. This is all so upsetting. First Zane is arrested and now this?"

Dakota listened as Zane filled them in on every thing, from the woman he'd never seen before showing up at his door for the bogus date, to the shooting last night at the old mission graveyard.

"This woman is your *sister?*" Hoyt asked, frowning. "I guess I never knew Clay had another daughter."

"Neither did I," Dakota said. She explained how she hadn't found out until her father's funeral.

"How old is this sister?" Emma asked, sounding as shocked as Dakota had felt.

"Not quite two years younger than me."

Hoyt got up and went to the cupboard over the sink. He pulled down a fresh bottle of bourbon and poured himself a drink, took a swig, then turned to ask if anyone else would like some.

"Hoyt, it's eight in the morning," Emma said, glad she'd dismissed Mrs. Crowley for the rest of the day. She'd hoped the housekeeper would go into town but as far as she knew, the woman had only gone as far as her room.

"How is it you never knew about this sister?" Hoyt

asked. His voice sounded strained as he ignored his wife's scolding.

Dakota explained about her father's affair. "It had to be about the time my mother was dying or right after."

"Thirty years ago," Hoyt said more to himself than to anyone in the kitchen. He finished his drink and poured himself another.

Emma got up and went to him, touching his arm. Dakota heard her whisper, "Are you okay, honey?"

He nodded and turned back to Dakota. "Did your sister say anything about her mother?"

"No, and I didn't ask. Then when she disappeared…"

Zane took up the story, explaining about the trip to Great Falls, meeting Camilla Hughes and finding out about Courtney's trip north.

"We think her birth mother contacted her because she was going by the last name of Baxter," Dakota said. "The mother's name was Lorraine Baxter."

All the color drained from Hoyt Chisholm's face. The glass in his hands slipped from his fingers. It hit the tile floor and shattered, glass shards skittering across the floor.

Emma let out a small startled cry as the glass broke at her husband's feet.

"What's wrong?" Emma cried as she grabbed his arm. He was visibly shaking, pale with beads of sweat breaking out on his forehead.

Dakota feared he was having a heart attack.

"Did you know her?" Zane asked as he stared at his father.

Hoyt swallowed. "I was married to her."

McCALL HAD PUT OFF CALLING Courtney Hughes's parents until she got the DNA test results from the blood found on the red dress she'd discovered under Zane Chisholm's bed.

She was anxious after everything that had happened. Zane Chisholm was adamant that he was being framed and Courtney and her birth mother were in on it. McCall didn't know what to believe. But she had a missing woman, an apparently abandoned car, evidence of possible foul play and two dead men.

The men had both been identified as escapees from a California prison. She had put a call in to the warden to see what she could find out about the men. Hopefully he might have some idea how they'd ended up in Montana, involved with Courtney Hughes aka Courtney Baxter.

When her phone rang, she jumped. The baby kicked as she reached for it. Just a few more days. In the meantime, she hoped to get some answers. She hated to leave this case for her undersheriff, who would be coming in cold on it.

She was relieved when she saw the call was from the state crime lab.

"The DNA found in the blond hair from the car matches the DNA found in the blood of the dress," the tech told her. "Same woman."

Time to call the young woman's parents.

"What was unusual," the tech continued, "was that the DNA search brought up a flagged comparison test from about thirty years ago."

"Flagged comparison test?"

"Another missing woman. This one was believed to have been drowned, but her DNA was sent to us and flagged in case any DNA test should produce a match."

Drowned, missing victim? McCall swallowed, her

heart pounding so hard she could barely hear herself think. "Are you telling me that a relative of Courtney Hughes is in the system?"

"Courtney Hughes's DNA results were a close enough match that the other one came up. Definitely related. I'd say mother and daughter. Interesting, huh?"

McCall thought about what Zane had told her. Courtney had been contacted by her birth mother. They suspected the Whitehorse Sewing Circle had been involved.

"You're saying that this other missing woman was Courtney's birth mother?"

"From the results, that is exactly what I'm saying. I pulled up the file. It's from a missing person's case from your area. A woman by the name of Laura Chisholm."

EMMA STARED AT HER HUSBAND. "There is another wife I don't know about?"

Hoyt shook his head and took her hands in his, his gaze filling with pain. "Lorraine Baxter was Laura Chisholm's maiden name. She thought 'Lorraine' sounded too old so she went by Laura. She had it changed legally, I think, at some point."

Everyone in the room fell silent as they let that sink in. Emma finally found her voice again.

"Courtney Hughes is Laura's daughter?" She looked over at Dakota. "You said she is about thirty-one or thirty-two? That means Courtney had to be born after Laura allegedly drowned," Emma said, even though she could see from everyone's faces that they'd all figured that out themselves.

Zane nodded. "So Laura Chisholm didn't drown, just as Aggie Wells said."

Emma felt sick to her stomach as she shooed her husband out of the way and cleaned up the broken glass. She needed the diversion. Her mind was spinning. Aggie had tried to warn her and now she was dead, all because no one had believed her. She reached behind her husband for the bourbon and poured herself a glass.

"I don't understand this," Hoyt said as he moved to the table and sat down heavily in one of the chairs. Some of his color had returned.

"It's pretty clear." Emma took a sip of the bourbon. It burned all the way down. "This is a message from Laura. All of this, setting up Zane, using Courtney— she wants you to know she's alive."

"Not just alive," Zane pointed out. "Capable of destroying our lives."

Hoyt rubbed a hand over his face. "Laura was so insecure, so needy. I was trying to build a ranch so I wasn't around enough. We were in the process of adopting the boys...."

"We have no proof that Laura is Courtney's mother," Emma said, knowing she was clutching at straws.

"I saw a birth certificate. It had both their names on it, but I suppose it could have been forged," Dakota said.

Hoyt shook his head. "Laura told me Clay was the father of her child."

Emma thought her husband couldn't surprise her further. She'd been wrong. She stared at him as if seeing a stranger. "When—"

"That day on the lake." He met her gaze. "I'm sorry I didn't tell you, but I couldn't bear to relive any more of the past than I've been forced to. Laura knew how badly I wanted a houseful of children. Her final blow was to tell me she was pregnant with Clay Lansing's baby."

"Did he know?" Dakota asked in a small voice.

"No. She told me she wasn't going to have it. I saw then that she had so little respect for human life and that was really the last straw. I told her I didn't love her and that I wanted a divorce. She went crazy."

"That's when she fell overboard," Emma said.

He nodded. "I wanted her out of my life but I didn't want her dead. I tried to save her...."

The room had fallen silent again.

Emma moved to her husband and wrapped her arms around him. "She's sick, obsessed and mentally unbalanced." None of those words came even close to describing Laura's kind of sickness.

"You realize we have no way of proving any of this," Zane said. "All we have is Camilla's word that the birth mother's name was Lorraine Baxter. Courtney has the birth certificate with both Lorraine's name and Clay Lansing's, and if Clay didn't know about the baby, then it is a forgery."

"She had the baby and gave it up for adoption?" Emma asked.

Dakota nodded. "We suspect through the Whitehorse Sewing Circle, so there will be no proof to find there."

"But surely one of the members..." Emma said. She'd heard about the group of women and what they'd done for years. It hadn't seemed like such a sinister thing to do, providing babies to good loving homes.

Now she feared that they might never know the truth. Unless Laura was found. She almost laughed at the thought. Laura would find them. She was probably close by, enjoying the pain she was causing them all.

"I'm worried about what she did to my sister," Dakota said.

"If we're right and Courtney is her daughter, then Laura wouldn't hurt her," Emma said with more conviction than she felt. Her words were met with silence.

Hoyt took her hand and squeezed it gently. "If Laura is alive, she's a murderer."

"How can you say *if?*" Emma demanded.

"Because I don't want to believe it," Hoyt said.

She softened her expression as she looked at him. Of course he didn't want to believe it. "Whatever she's done, it has nothing to do with you."

His laugh held no humor. "Emma, it has everything to do with me. I'm at fault. She didn't believe that I loved her enough. She turned to another man. Everything she's done is because I failed her."

"The woman is insane," Zane snapped. "You just happened to be the man she became obsessed with."

Dakota hadn't spoken for a while. When she did, everyone turned to look at her because of the anguish they heard in her voice.

"I think Laura might be responsible for my father's death," Dakota said. "I was so hurt that Courtney was with him when he died and not me...." Her gaze came up. Her eyes welled with tears. "If Courtney was with our father when he died, then it was her mother's doing. I wouldn't be surprised if Laura was there when he had his heart attack. I can only imagine my father's reaction to finding out what Laura had done and meeting a daughter he hadn't known existed."

Zane put his arm around her as a vehicle pulled up outside.

Emma glanced out the window and felt her stomach roil with dread. "It's the sheriff."

Z ANE OPENED THE DOOR at the sheriff's knock, worried that she was here to take him back to jail.

"Sheriff Crawford," he said, hoping he was wrong because he couldn't leave Dakota, wouldn't leave her without a fight.

"Zane. I need to have a word with your father. Is he—" McCall looked past him.

"Please come in," Hoyt said. Zane moved aside to let her enter the house.

The sheriff glanced at Dakota, then Emma, and said, "I'm glad you're all here. I have some news on the DNA test the crime lab ran on Courtney Hughes's blood sample."

"Please sit down," Emma said. "Can I get you—"

"Nothing, thank you." She sat down and waited for everyone else to sit as well.

"Apparently when your first wife drowned, you gave the crime lab a sample of her DNA?" McCall asked Hoyt.

He nodded. Zane noticed how he stole a glance at Emma. They all seemed to know what was coming.

"The crime lab in Missoula ran Courtney's DNA. It brought up another close match. Laura Chisholm's," the sheriff said. "It appears that Courtney Hughes is Laura Chisholm's daughter."

She looked to Hoyt. He said nothing. They'd wanted confirmation. Now they had it.

"You already knew this?" the sheriff asked, looking around the room at them.

"We just learned that Laura Chisholm was Lorraine Baxter before she married my father," Zane said. "We hadn't known that she was definitely Courtney's birth mother."

"I don't think I have to tell you what this means," McCall said. "If Zane is right, then Laura Chisholm is behind her daughter's disappearance."

"She orchestrated all of this," Emma said.

The sheriff shook her head. "The only thing we're lacking is proof of that."

"She's not finished with this family," Hoyt said, his voice breaking with emotion.

"You have to find her," Emma said. "If she's using her own daughter to hurt my family…"

"I'm circulating copies of that age-progression photo Aggie Wells gave you not only locally, but also throughout the state," McCall said. "I'm doing everything possible to find her *and Courtney*." She didn't need to add, "If she is still alive." Everyone in the room had to be thinking the same thing.

"I'll make sure Emma is never alone," Hoyt said. "I'll have one of the boys stay with her as well as Mrs. Crowley."

The sheriff's cell phone rang. She glanced at it. "I need to take this." She got to her feet and stepped out of the room.

A few moments later, she came back into the room. Zane saw the expression on her face and felt his heart drop.

"Is it Courtney?" Dakota asked before anyone else could speak.

McCall shook her head. "That was the warden at the prison in California where the two dead men did time. Both are escaped criminals." She seemed to hesitate. "Three prisoners walked away from a work area last week."

"Three?" Zane said.

"The warden said they'd all three had a visitor a few weeks before. He described her as a woman in her late fifties to early sixties, blonde, blue-eyed. She was going by the name of Sharon Jones and used a Billings, Montana, address."

"Sharon Jones? The woman Aggie found and swore was Laura Chisholm," Emma cried.

"What more proof do you want that this whole thing is some sort of vengeance against our family?" Zane demanded.

"Until she is caught, all of you need to be very careful," McCall said. "There's a third man out there, not to mention Laura herself. I think everything going on with Zane is merely a diversion to bring the focus off the real target, Emma."

The sheriff turned to look at Emma. "If we're right and Laura is responsible for Hoyt's other wives' deaths, then Laura will be coming after you."

Chapter Eleven

Dakota was still stunned by everything that had happened in the past forty-eight hours.

"I'm not letting you out of my sight until this is over," Zane said as they left the Chisholm ranch.

She smiled over at him. His words were music to her ears. He'd saved her at the cemetery, risked his life. She couldn't help but think about the kiss as they went back to her ranch where she packed up what she would need.

From there, they drove back toward Whitehorse. "We can stay out at the home ranch with my folks, but I need to go by my place first."

She didn't say anything as they pulled into the yard of his house. There were no other vehicles around—just like at her house. She reminded herself that Courtney's car had been found.

But the third escaped prisoner from California was still at large. She wanted to believe that by now he had crossed the border into Canada and was long gone. Believing that Courtney and her mother had also skipped the country was a little harder to swallow.

"Doesn't look like anyone has been here," Zane said as he unlocked the door and stepped inside. "If you just give me a minute…"

"Zane." He stopped and turned to look at her, concern in his expression.

She stepped up to him and pushed a lock of his blond hair back from his handsome face. "Thank you."

He shook his head. "I got you into this."

"No, this started long before us. I just want to thank you. You saved my life last night."

His gaze locked with hers. "Dakota." The word came out like a prayer. She felt warmth rush through her. "Don't you know by now how I feel about you? I was half in love with that kid you used to be. Now..." He shook his head as if he couldn't put what he felt into words.

She leaned toward him and brushed her lips over his.

He drew back. "You sure about this?"

Had she ever been more sure of anything in her life? And yet, she knew that this would change everything between them—and possibly not for the better.

She'd taken chances in her life, plenty of them, but that was on the back of a horse in an arena or with the rough stock business. This was a whole different matter and she knew she was way out of her league.

He brushed her cheek with the rough pads of his fingertips, turning her face up to his so she couldn't avoid his blue gaze. She saw the cool blue and the heat behind it. With Zane Chisholm it would be all or nothing.

She nodded slowly and his hand slid behind her head, his fingers burying themselves in her long hair. He pulled her toward him until his mouth hovered over hers. Her breasts pressed against his hard chest, and his hold was strong and sure.

Her heart pounded like a war drum as he drew back

to meet her gaze again, as if searching for something to stop this before it got out of hand.

She met that steely gaze with one of her own. The one thing she had never lacked was courage. Those long-ago embers now fanned to a flame so hot she felt her blood catch fire.

Funny how nothing had changed and yet everything had. She was no longer that girl. He'd said men were going to want to kiss her. And they had. Just none of them had been Zane Chisholm. Until now.

His mouth dropped to hers in a stunning kiss that left her breathless. "That has been a long time coming," Zane said, sounding just as breathless.

She realized why he hadn't kissed her all those years ago. Nothing about Zane Chisholm was safe. She was just smart enough to know it now.

Zane swung her up in his arms, kicked open his bedroom door and carried her inside. As he laid her on the covers, she wrapped her arms around his neck and pulled him down, unable to go another moment without kissing him.

When she touched his lower lip with the tip of her tongue, she felt a shudder rock through him. With a curse he let her pull him down to the bed.

For a moment he stared down at her as if seeing her for the woman she'd become instead of that cowgirl she'd been.

Then he dropped his mouth on hers, taking possession of it, stealing her senses and proving that his earlier kiss was only a prelude of what was to come.

He grabbed her Western shirt and pulled the two sides apart with a jerk that made the snaps sing. A moan escaped his lips as he gazed down at her breasts straining against the lace fabric.

He undid the front hook with two fingers and she felt her breasts freed. His gaze took them in, then those blue eyes shifted to her face.

"You are so beautiful," he said, his voice sounding hoarse. He lowered himself to the bed beside her, his fingers brushing one hard nipple and making her shiver with a desire she knew only he could quench.

His mouth dropped to the other breast and she arched against him, silently pleading with him not to stop.

He trailed kisses, damp and sweet, over her body, making her wriggle in pleasurable agony until at last he shed his jeans and she felt the heat of his body against hers.

He took her in his arms and slowly made love to her with ever-deepening kisses. The release came like a train gathering speed. She clung to him, crying out as she felt wave after wave of ecstasy.

Zane collapsed next to her, his hand spread on her damp stomach. They lay like that, breathing hard, both of them knowing they wouldn't be going to the Chisholm home ranch tonight.

EMMA HAD A TERRIBLE TIME getting to sleep. Zane had called to say that he and Dakota were staying at his place. Emma hadn't argued. She'd smiled as she'd hung up the phone. It was clear Zane was crazy about the girl.

And to think that a year ago, Emma had thought she was going to have to help her stepsons find the perfect women for them. Somehow they'd all done it on their own. She guessed that was the way it was meant to be.

Of course, each of them had fallen in love with a

woman in trouble. So typical of Chisholm men, she'd thought as she'd climbed into bed next to Hoyt.

It was a little after two when she woke. She slipped out of bed and went to the window. The pickup Mrs. Crowley used was gone. Earlier, the housekeeper had complained of a headache and gone to her room. Which had relieved both Emma and Hoyt. They didn't really want her to know what was going on.

But apparently Mrs. Crowley had felt well enough later to go out after Emma and Hoyt had gone to bed.

"What are you doing?" Hoyt asked from the bed, making Emma jump.

"I couldn't sleep," she said when she found her voice. She didn't want him to know she was spying on their housekeeper. He'd think she had enough problems without that.

He blinked. "So you are just sitting in the dark?"

"Go back to sleep. I like sitting here. If it bothers you, maybe I'll go downstairs and read for a while."

"You sure you're all right?" he asked, sounding worried.

"I'm fine." She got up and went to the bed, leaning in to kiss him. "Go to sleep. I'll be back before you know it."

He smiled and closed his eyes. "You can read up here—I don't mind the light."

"I left my book downstairs." She waited for him to put up more of an argument but a moment later she heard him snoring softly.

As she crept downstairs, she admitted that spying on her housekeeper helped keep her mind off Laura Chisholm. But she knew that was only partly the truth.

Mrs. Crowley was too smug in her secrets. Emma was determined to solve this one.

Moving to the living room window, she didn't dare turn on a light. Mrs. Crowley might see it. Instead, she sat patiently in the dark, hoping Hoyt didn't awaken again and come looking for her.

Twenty minutes later, she saw headlights in the distance.

Emma waited another five minutes after Mrs. Crowley had parked the pickup and gone inside her wing before tiptoeing into the kitchen for the flashlight and spare truck key.

She knew she wasn't being as careful, but she had to put an end to this nightly spying. With the key and flashlight, she padded out of the kitchen, across the living room and out the front door.

It was colder out tonight. The sky was dark and the wind smelled of rain. She hurried along the side of the house in the shadows, feeling the bite of the wind. Rain was imminent.

It would serve her right to get wet, she thought as she slipped around the back of the pickup and through the passenger side door. If Hoyt caught her drenched in rain, how was she going to explain that?

This time, she didn't take the time to wait and see if anyone might have seen her. She turned the key and snapped on the flashlight.

The beam shone on the odometer reading.

Emma blinked and did quick subtraction. Eleven miles? Eleven miles round-trip, she realized. That meant the woman hadn't even left the ranch.

It was more puzzling than when she hadn't known

how far away the woman went in the middle of the night.

And more troubling somehow.

Rain pinged off the truck roof, making her jump. She hurriedly climbed out, slamming the door harder than she meant to.

Thunder rumbled in the distance. She hoped anyone who might have heard the slammed door would think that was what it had been.

As she started around the truck, a bolt of lightning splintered across the sky, lighting up the yard like daylight.

For a moment, Emma was blinded. She blinked and when her eyes focused again, she found herself face-to-face with Mrs. Crowley.

DAKOTA WOKE TO THUNDER that was so close it seemed to reverberate inside her chest. In the darkness she shivered and rolled over to face Zane. His features were lit by the light of the storm. He couldn't have looked more handsome than he did right now, she thought with a growing ache inside her.

Earlier she'd gotten up to get a drink and had pulled on his T-shirt. It smelled of him, filling her senses. As she'd slipped it over her head, her skin had tingled. Now she remembered the way the T-shirt had fit him, accenting the hard muscles, the washboard stomach, the tanned skin. She couldn't help but remember the way his jeans had hung on his hips, the fine blond line of hair that ran from his chest to disappear at the large rodeo belt buckle.

She had looked away, but not before he'd seen her

looking. A fire had burned in those blue eyes, hot as a welder's torch.

At just the thought of their lovemaking, she felt a fire burning in her. She'd never known this kind of passion, this kind of desire. Zane had been her childhood fantasy, the rodeo cowboy she'd planned to marry.

At the thought of her diary, she cringed inwardly. It embarrassed her that her sister, and who knew who else, had read about her longing. No doubt the reason it still embarrassed her was because that longing had never gone away.

Zane was the reason she hadn't gone through with her engagement. She'd felt as if there was something missing with her fiancé. Dakota had hated breaking it off, telling herself she was making a huge mistake still being in love with a fantasy cowboy.

But the truth was, Zane had corralled her heart and held it captive all these years.

In a flash of lightning that lit the bedroom, Zane opened his eyes. He smiled at her. "Nice shirt," he said.

Raindrops struck the partially open window next to them. Dakota felt the cool breeze rush over her bare skin as she brushed her lips over his, then pulled back a little to look at him. He seemed to be waiting to see how far she would go.

She shifted against Zane, feeling her aching nipples grow even harder beneath his T-shirt as she reached for the hem. Pulling his T-shirt up and over her head, she tossed it away.

He grinned. "You are insatiable."

She nodded as she wrapped her arms around his neck and pressed her naked breasts to his hard chest.

His hands came around her waist and drew her into

him until not even the cool breeze of the rainstorm could come between them. As his mouth dropped to hers, thunder boomed again as loud as the pounding of their hearts in the old ranch house.

"MRS. CROWLEY!" THE words flew from Emma's mouth with obvious surprise.

"Whatever are you doing standing out in the rain?" the woman demanded from beneath the umbrella she held.

Emma had been so careful the other time. Now she'd been caught red handed. "The thunder and lightning. It woke me up."

Mrs. Crowley was giving her a sideways look that said, "And that explains your behavior how?"

"I woke up, couldn't sleep and wandered out on the porch. I thought I saw the dome light on in the pickup," Emma said. It was the only thing she could think of since she was pretty sure Mrs. Crowley had seen her in the truck.

"Really? Do you have trouble sleeping often?"

"Must have been the thunder," Emma said.

Mrs. Crowley glanced toward the pickup. "The dome light must have a short in it. I noticed it wasn't working the other night."

So she *had* noticed. Of course she had, Emma thought. The woman never missed anything.

"I'll have Hoyt take a look at it," Emma said.

"Don't bother. It's off now. Let's just leave it that way." Mrs. Crowley gave her one of her twisted half smiles. "You really should get in out of the rain."

With that the woman turned and went back inside.

Emma stood for a moment, staring after her before she turned her face up to the rain. It felt good as she walked back to the front porch before entering the house.

Inside, she locked the door. Even as she did so she wondered what she was locking inside her house.

She shuddered at the memory of looking up to find Mrs. Crowley standing in front of her. Why did that poor woman scare her so?

Well, she'd never admit it. Especially to Hoyt.

Eleven miles, she thought as she went to the guest bathroom and dried herself off with a towel. Hoyt's robe was soaked. She hung it up.

Her nightgown was damp. She would change it upstairs.

As she headed upstairs, she mulled it over in her mind. Eleven miles round-trip. Where would that take you on the ranch?

Upset with herself, she knew she really *wouldn't* be able to sleep now. Retracing her steps, she went into the living room, turned on a lamp and picked up the murder mystery she'd been reading.

She was through spying on the poor woman, she told herself as she wrote down the mileage in the back of the book and wondered again where an eleven-mile round-trip would take a person on the Chisholm ranch.

THE NEXT MORNING THE STORM had passed. A brilliant glowing sun shone in the window from a sky of cloudless blue. Zane stirred to find the bed beside him empty. For one heart-stopping moment, he thought Dakota was gone.

Then he smelled bacon and heard the faint sound of music coming from his radio in the kitchen. He smiled and tried to still his pounding heart. Last night had been incredible. What surprised him was that it hadn't been like this with other women he'd known. He knew it sounded clichéd, but with Dakota it hadn't been just sex.

As he lay in the bed, it hit him like a boulder off a cliff. He loved her.

He'd never said the *L* word to any woman because he'd never loved any of them. For a few moments, he was shocked. But he realized this wasn't a spur-of-the-moment emotion. This had been coming for a long time.

Pulling on his jeans, he looked around for his T-shirt. Not seeing it, he grinned. He had a pretty good idea where he could find it.

Sure enough, as he stepped through the kitchen doorway, there was Dakota making breakfast in nothing but his T-shirt.

He moved behind her, put his arms around her, breathed in the scent of bacon and the woman he loved.

"I hope you're hungry," she said with a sexy chuckle.

"Hmm," he said into the side of her neck. She felt warm and soft, rounded in all the right places. He loved her strength as much as he loved her soft places.

Turning off the stove, he turned her in his arms. "What would it take to get you to come back to bed with me?"

EMMA HAD SLEPT. She woke sprawled on the couch with a crick in her neck and a page of her murder mystery pressed against her right cheek.

At first she didn't know what had roused her. Then she heard the phone and realized it wasn't the first time it had rung.

Still in her nightgown, she hurried to it, aware that it must be very early. Not even Mrs. Crowley was up yet.

"I just got a call from the Butte Police Department," Sheriff McCall Crawford said when Emma answered. "They've picked up a woman who matches Laura's description from the age-progression photo we sent around the region."

Emma couldn't help being afraid to get her hopes up. She'd prayed for this for so long. "But they aren't sure?"

"No, but they did find some evidence in her possession that makes them believe it's her," the sheriff said. "She had Courtney's number and Great Falls address on her and some gas receipts from a Westside convenience store in Whitehorse."

"Are they going to bring her to Whitehorse?"

"No," McCall said. "They need Hoyt to come to Butte to make a positive identification. They can only hold her for forty-eight hours so he needs to come as soon as possible."

Hoyt would have to face his first wife? Emma couldn't bear him having to do that. But if this was Laura and they couldn't hold her any longer because of lack of evidence...

"I'll tell Hoyt." She hung up and hurried upstairs only to find their bed empty. Hurrying back downstairs, she checked the kitchen and then headed for the barn.

She found him with his horses—the place he always headed when he was worried or upset. So he hadn't been able to sleep after all, she thought, wondering how long he'd been out there.

Emma watched him brushing one of his favorite horses. She could hear him talking softly to the mare and felt such a rush of love for him it almost floored her.

She took a step toward him, hating to interrupt. He looked so peaceful and she knew that this news would kill that instantly.

"Emma?" Hoyt seemed surprised to see her. "I thought you'd be asleep for hours." He smiled, making it clear he'd seen her sacked out on the couch. She probably still had the crease on her cheek where the page of her book had been pressed.

"I just got a call from the sheriff," she said. Hoyt put down the brush and stepped toward her. She quickly repeated what McCall had told her and watched an array of emotions cross his face.

"Then it's her," Hoyt said, sounding so relieved she stepped to him and put her arms around him. He pulled her close and she could hear the ragged emotion in his voice as he breathed words of love into her hair.

"I have been so worried about you, Emma," he said when she pulled back. "I have to go to Butte today? Why can't they just check her DNA since it is still on file?"

"I don't know. Apparently it would take too long. Or maybe she refused to take a DNA test. I hate for you to have to go, but if this woman is Laura…"

"Yes," he said. "It definitely sounds like she is. I'll do whatever I have to. I just want this to be over."

"Me, too," Emma said. She thought they would all be able to breathe again once Laura was locked up for good.

"I'll call one of the boys to stay with you until I get back," he said. Hoyt still referred to his sons as boys, even though they were all almost thirty or older.

She started to argue that it wasn't necessary. She had Mrs. Crowley. But her husband didn't give her a chance.

"I'd feel better if one of our sons is here with you until I'm positive they have Laura behind bars. Let's not forget that there is a third prison escapee still on the loose."

She hadn't forgotten. But with Laura locked up, she doubted they had to worry about the other escapee. By now he could already be across the border into Canada.

Chapter Twelve

Zane swore at the sound of the phone. He thought about not answering it. Right now the last thing he wanted was an intrusion from the outside world.

He glanced over at Dakota on the bed next to him. Her body felt so warm next to his, he never wanted to leave this bed.

The phone rang again. He reached for it and checked to see who was calling. When he saw that it was the ranch he quickly slipped out of bed.

He answered on the third ring. "Hello?"

"Zane, it's Dad." Zane listened as he filled him in about the trip to Butte and the woman the police there had behind bars. "Marshall is going to be staying with Emma, but I wanted the rest of you to know what's going on."

"They really think it's her?"

"Apparently she had Courtney's number and address on her and some gas receipts from the Westside here in Whitehorse."

"Then she'll be able to tell the police where Courtney is," Zane said, and heard Dakota come up beside him. She was wearing his shirt again and nothing else.

At this rate, they were never going to eat the breakfast she'd cooked.

"Let me know what happens." He hung up to take Dakota in his arms and tell her the possible good news.

"Has this woman they arrested said anything about Courtney yet?"

"Apparently not. But she did have Courtney's address and phone number and some gas receipts from Whitehorse."

Dakota snuggled against him, wrapping her arms around his waist and burying her face into his bare chest.

"Dad promised to call when he knew something definite."

She pulled back to look up at him. "I'm just so afraid that the more time that goes by…"

"I know." He thought about Courtney's car being found in that ravine—and one of the escaped prisoners' bodies found nearby. He regretted that he'd had to kill the other escaped convict last night before finding out anything about Courtney.

Zane swung Dakota up into his arms and carried her back to the bedroom. Putting her down gently, he lay beside her on the bed.

She was so beautiful. He touched her face, running his thumb pad over her smooth cheek. Her eyes widened and he saw desire stir in them.

"If we don't eat that wonderful breakfast you cooked pretty soon…"

HOYT REFUSED TO LEAVE until Marshall arrived. Emma was relieved when she saw Marshall drive up and Hoyt go out to talk to him. She and Hoyt had already said their goodbyes. She could tell Hoyt was just anxious to get to Butte.

A pilot friend had offered to fly him and was now waiting for him at the small airport outside of White-horse. It was no more than a wind sock, a strip of tarmac and an old metal hangar. But by flying, Hoyt could get there sooner—and get back just as quickly.

"Where's Mrs. Crowley?" Marshall whispered as he came through the back door and looked around the kitchen. Emma waved out the window to Hoyt as he climbed into his pickup. His gaze locked with hers for a moment before he started the motor and drove away.

"She wasn't feeling well and went to her room to rest," Emma said, turning from the window. "I'm worried about her. This isn't like her. But I don't dare go down to her room. She called me to say she had one of her headaches and asked if I would mind if she stayed in bed a little longer."

"She must have known I was coming over," he said. "She doesn't like me."

"That's not true," Emma said. He raised a brow and she laughed. "She doesn't like anyone," Emma whispered conspiratorially. "Sit down. I baked your second-most favorite cookies."

"I thought I smelled lemon." He smiled and slid into a chair at the table. "Dad eat all the gingersnaps?"

Emma closed the kitchen door so they would have privacy and turned on the radio to the country music station.

"Mrs. Crowley hates this kind of music," she said as she gave him a mug of hot coffee and a plate of lemon cookies and took a chair across from him.

He grinned at her. "How can you stand her?"

"Well…" She studied her stepson for a moment. "Can I tell you something? You just can't tell your father what I've been doing."

He made a cross with his finger over his heart and laughed. "If you've been slipping Mrs. Crowley happy pills, I've got some bad news for you. They aren't workin'."

Emma shook her head and leaned toward him. "I've been spying on her. And guess what? She sneaks off at night after we're asleep and she doesn't come back until the wee hours of the morning."

He frowned, clearly not expecting this. "Where does she go?"

"Well, that's what's so interesting. She only drives eleven miles, round-trip."

"That wouldn't even get her off the ranch."

"Exactly. But I think I've figured out where she goes. I just can't imagine why…unless she's meeting some man—" Emma realized "—at the old water mill house."

Emma realized Marshall wasn't listening to her anymore. He was looking past her out the kitchen window one moment, the next he was shooting to his feet, a curse escaping his lips.

She spun around to look out the window behind her, half expecting to see Mrs. Crowley's face pressed to the glass.

"Fire," Marshall said reaching for his cell phone. "Grass fire."

Emma saw it then. Smoke on the horizon. She'd learned about grass fires since moving to the ranch and knew how dangerous they could be, especially if pushed by wind. Outside the window she could see a brisk wind stirring the branches of the cottonwood trees.

She listened to Marshall barking information into the phone. He placed five more calls to his brothers.

"Go," she said when he snapped his phone shut. "I'm fine. Mrs. Crowley is here."

Marshall shook his head. "Zane is bringing Dakota to stay with you."

Emma liked Dakota and would be glad to spend some time with her. "Well, you don't have to wait for them to get here. Mrs. Crowley is in her room and I have your number if I have to reach you. You'll only be down the road."

The kitchen door suddenly opened. "What's going on?" Mrs. Crowley asked as she filled the doorway.

"Are you feeling better?" Emma asked.

"What's going on? I heard all the racket," the housekeeper said in answer.

"There's a grass fire. The boys have gone to fight it."

Mrs. Crowley went to the window and looked out as if she'd known where it was, had already seen it. "So what are you waiting for?" she demanded as she turned to face Marshall. "Shouldn't you be out there fighting it?"

He didn't get a chance to reply.

"I'm here with your stepmother now," Mrs. Crowley said in her no-nonsense tone. "Go."

"She's right," Emma said. "We'll be fine."

Marshall didn't have to be told twice. "Dakota is going to drop off Zane, then come here. She should be here soon," he said. "Call if you need me."

"I will," Emma said as she pushed him out the door. He took off running toward the ranch truck with the water tank on the back. A few minutes later, he was roaring down the road toward the dark smudge of smoke along the horizon.

"Marshall didn't even eat one of the cookies I made for him," Emma said. She turned to find Mrs. Crowley making tea.

"YOU MUST BE FEELING BETTER," Emma said, looking out the window at the fire.

Mrs. Crowley could hear the woman's fear about the fire, but it was so like Emma to ask how *she* was feeling.

"I am better, thank you." Her employer turned in surprise at her words. "I appreciate how nice you've been to me. I know I haven't made it easy."

Emma's eyes widened a little as if she wasn't sure the words had really come out of her housekeeper's mouth.

Mrs. Crowley nodded, not having to pretend a look of chagrin. "You have been nothing but kind and I have rebuffed that kindness at every turn. I'm sorry."

Emma appeared not to know what to say for a moment. "I just wanted you to feel at home here. I have a tendency to come on too strong."

"I do feel at home here." Emma had no idea how much. "Please, let me make us a cup of tea and visit until your friend gets here."

"Are you sure you feel up to making the tea?"

"Yes. I only had a headache earlier. I'm fine now." She turned her back on Emma and began to fill the teapot, hoping the woman would take a seat and not insist on helping.

To her relief, Emma was more interested in the grass fire.

Mrs. Crowley tried not to hurry with the tea but

time was of the essence. Dakota Lansing would be arriving soon. She had to get at least one cup of tea into Emma before that. This opportunity might not present itself again.

"I suppose you won't be needing me soon," Mrs. Crowley said.

"Why would you say that?" Emma asked.

"Your husband's trip to Butte. I couldn't help overhearing. Is it really possible his first wife is alive?"

"I'm afraid so."

Mrs. Crowley shook her head as the teapot whistled. "I admit I did read a few things in the newspaper before I came here. I felt as if you and I had a lot in common actually. We are both haunted in a way by the past."

"That's true," Emma agreed as she poured a small pitcher of milk and prepared the cups.

"What I can't understand is why this woman would do what she's been accused of." She carefully filled Emma's cup and slipped in a fresh tea bag. "She must enjoy making other people miserable," she said as she watched the tea steep.

"I feel sorry for her," Emma said and Mrs. Crowley had to bite back a laugh. Of course Emma would.

"How can you possibly say that?" she demanded as she slipped a tea bag into her own cup, then took both cups over to the table, making sure she didn't accidentally mix them up as she saw the dust of a vehicle coming up the road in the distance.

"She must be a very unhappy person," Emma said.

"Maybe she just couldn't let go of her husband," Mrs. Crowley said as she pulled out a chair and sat down across from her. "Isn't it possible she loved him too much? That he was her life and she didn't need anything or anyone else?"

Emma took a sip of her tea and looked up in surprise. "You think she resented the children he adopted?"

Mrs. Crowley shrugged and sipped at her tea, watching Emma over the rim of her cup.

"I think she didn't want him but she doesn't want anyone else to have him," Emma said, then took one of the lemon cookies off the plate on the table and dipped it into the tea. She took a bite, then said, "That is the most selfish of all love."

EMMA DIDN'T LIKE THE TASTE of the tea and wondered how Mrs. Crowley could mess up even a simple cup of tea.

The woman was no cook. If Emma'd had her way, she wouldn't have let her in the kitchen. Every time Mrs. Crowley insisted on helping, nothing had turned out like it should have.

Emma prided herself on her cooking, especially her baking. Fortunately, Mrs. Crowley hadn't insisted on helping with the baking.

She took another sip of the tea. It tasted bitter. She tried not to grimace with the woman watching her.

"I think I need a little of that sweetener my future daughters-in-law insist on," Emma said.

Mrs. Crowley was being so nice, she rose quickly to get it.

Emma used the diversion to dump some of the tea out in the plant on the windowsill. She would have poured out more but Mrs. Crowley was too quick for her.

"Thank you," she said as she took one of the packets, tore it open and poured it into her cup under Mrs. Crowley's watchful eye.

Emma hated sweetener, but she had no choice now but to drink the tea. Mrs. Crowley knew she didn't take her tea with milk, but she added a little anyway, hoping it would make the brew go down easier.

Mrs. Crowley was making an effort to be friends. Too late if the woman in Butte turned out to be Laura. Emma would feel badly about having to let Mrs. Crowley go. Well, not that badly. She would never know, though, where the housekeeper went in the middle of the night.

Emma promised herself that she would give Mrs. Crowley a decent recommendation for her next job and make Hoyt give her a large severance package.

Even as she thought it, Emma knew she probably wouldn't have done that if the woman wasn't disfigured. She wondered if Mrs. Crowley was often overly compensated by her employers not for her work but because of her injury. Emma supposed that, too, could have made the woman the way she was.

Or at least had been. She'd been so pleasant today it was almost…spooky. Emma could feel Mrs. Crowley studying her. Now that she thought about it, many times since the housekeeper had arrived here she'd felt her studying her like a bug under a magnifying glass.

Another benefit of her injury, Emma thought vaguely. No one dared stare at Mrs. Crowley, which made it easier for her to stare at everyone else.

Emma put down her cup. She'd been forced to drink all but a little of it. She suddenly felt light-headed. She could barely keep her eyes open.

MRS. CROWLEY CONCENTRATED on her tea, letting Emma drink almost all of hers. A breeze stirred at the open kitchen window, bringing with it the smell of smoke. Hoyt was in Butte and by now all the Chisholm boys would be fighting the fire.

But the wind also carried the scent of dust. As she listened, Mrs. Crowley heard the vehicle she'd seen down the road approaching. It was only a matter of minutes before it reached the ranch house.

Mrs. Crowley glanced toward the window and the pickup that pulled into the yard. It was just a neighbor coming to refill the water tank in the back of his truck.

She looked over at Emma again. There was still time.

Emma was staring into her teacup as if reading her future in the small sprinkling of leaves at the bottom.

All things considered, not much of a future, Mrs. Crowley thought.

"I think Laura was scarred in ways none of us will ever understand," she said. "Did you know that her father deserted her when she was six? He was her life. Her mother remarried, of course, after transforming herself into whatever that man wanted her to be. The marriages never lasted so she kept having to become someone new for someone else."

Emma looked up and blinked as if having a hard time focusing.

"Laura's mother cared more about the men who traipsed through the house in a steady flow than she ever did about her daughter," Mrs. Crowley continued as she rose to take Emma's cup.

"You wouldn't know what it's like growing up feeling that you're not enough, that your love isn't valuable enough, that you're not even enough for your own mother. But I think you can imagine what something like that can do to a person," Mrs. Crowley said.

SOMETHING WAS WRONG. Emma had been trying to follow the conversation but Mrs. Crowley's words weren't making any sense.

She stared across the table at the woman. Mrs. Crowley looked different this morning, but Emma couldn't put her finger on what it was. She reached for a cookie, but hit the small pitcher of milk. Milk splashed onto the table.

"Here, let me help you with that," the housekeeper said, moving the pitcher out of her reach.

"I'm not feeling well." Her head was spinning and she could barely keep her eyes open.

"You must have what I did earlier. Headache? Lightheadedness? I was so tired I could barely stay awake."

Emma looked into the woman's face and had a moment of clarity. "Did you put something in my tea?"

Mrs. Crowley smiled. "It's all right. I only gave you a very strong sedative. It will knock you out, but it won't kill you. That comes later."

Emma tried to stand, but the housekeeper was on her before she could get out of the chair. She struggled to throw her off, but Mrs. Crowley was much stronger than she looked.

Nor was she limping, Emma thought as the housekeeper half dragged her toward the pantry. She gave up fighting to free herself from the woman's grip, realizing it was useless.

She was too weak. But she still fought to stay awake. Dakota was on her way. If she called out—

Emma opened her mouth, but only a low groan came out as the housekeeper dragged her into the pantry.

Emma's eyelids drooped and the last thing she heard as she lay on the floor was the hurried slamming of the pantry door. Then darkness.

MRS. CROWLEY LOOKED DOWN the road. No Dakota yet. She sat down, poured a little milk into her tea and idly stirred it with her spoon. It was dangerous, this game she was playing. She had let it go on too long. She'd been in this house since March. It was now June and she hadn't accomplished what she'd come here to do.

With a curse, she knew why it had taken her so long. Emma. The woman had intrigued her. Each day she'd relished watching her employer. Emma had an insatiable curiosity and a need to comfort. Mrs. Crowley smiled at the woman's pitiful attempts to befriend her.

The curiosity could have turned out to be a problem, though. While she was watching Emma, Emma had been spying on her. She chuckled to herself at Emma's attempts to find out where she'd gone at night. Taking a sip of tea, she almost spilled it as she recalled Emma's face when she'd caught her coming out of the cab of the pickup last night.

Feeling good for the first time in a long time, Mrs. Crowley considered having one of Emma's cookies. Normally she didn't allow herself the pleasure of sweets. She had just taken a bite when she heard the sound of a vehicle. Looking out the kitchen window, she saw the driver of the pickup park in front of the house and climb from behind the wheel.

Dakota Lansing. Before the other night, she hadn't

seen her since she was a cute little two-year-old, Clay Lansing's pride and joy.

She watched the now beautiful young woman head for the front door and felt a stab of remorse. Clay Lansing never knew it, but she could have fallen for him all those years ago. There was something so broken about him after his wife died. She'd been drawn to his pain and thrown caution to the wind.

She would have left Hoyt for Clay if it hadn't been for Dakota. It was ironic. She hadn't wanted a child, and in her reckless abandon had become pregnant with one.

She listened, but no sound came from inside the pantry. Smiling, she went to answer the knock at the door.

THE FIRE HAD RACED ACROSS the prairie, fueled by the wind and the tall grasses, and left charred, black ground. Smoke still billowed up along the horizon and could be seen for miles, but the flames had been knocked down.

This was the wrong time of the year for grass fires. Unfortunately an early spring, hot temperatures and abundant grass had kept the blaze going.

When Zane arrived he found his brothers, along with neighbors who had seen the smoke and come to help. They'd managed to get the fire contained and were now busy dousing any grass and brush still smoking.

Another truck pulled in equipped with a water tank in the bed. Zane saw that his brothers had almost emptied their tanks and would need to make a run back to the ranch to refill soon unless they got the fire completely out with this last tank of water.

Zane backed up his pickup and jumped out to grab the hose from the back and turn on the faucet of the water tank. The spray felt cold and blew back in his face as he began to douse the grass along the edge of where the fire had burned. Down the way, more neighbors were working along with several small community volunteer fire department crews.

Zane was thankful that his brothers were already winning the battle against the blaze. What he wanted to know now was how it could have started out here in the middle of nowhere—especially after a rain last night. Unless it had been started by a lightning strike and taken this long to get going.

After emptying the tank in the back of the truck, Zane moved across the blackened ground to the spot where the blaze appeared to have started. He hadn't gone far when he saw the containers of accelerant and the boot prints in the soft earth.

Hunkering down, he studied the track and then, on an impulse, looked to the horizon where the foothills rose in small clusters of pines. Zane caught a flash of light in the pines along the foothills not a half mile away.

Binoculars, he thought. The arsonist is watching to see how much damage he's caused.

A moment later Zane realized the arsonist had seen him and knew he'd been spotted. A pickup roared out of the trees in the distance. The driver was making a run for it.

Swearing, Zane sprinted for one of the ranch trucks. The bastard wasn't getting away.

As he neared the truck, Zane called to his brothers. "The man who started the fire. I saw him watching us from the trees. He's taking off."

Zane jumped behind the wheel. His brother Marshall

climbed into the passenger side as the truck engine roared to life, and Zane swung it around and headed for the county road to cut the man off.

Dust billowed up behind them as they raced across the pasture. Zane could see the blue pickup's driver careening down the road, hoping to escape before Zane could catch him.

"Can't this pickup go any faster?" Marshall joked, hanging on as the truck bounced over the ruts, fishtailing onto the road.

For a moment it looked as if the blue pickup would beat them to the spot where the two roads joined.

Zane feared that if the driver of the blue truck got there first, he might be able to outrun them. After all, his truck didn't have a water tank in the back.

He pushed the pickup harder, keeping his eye on the road as he and the other driver raced toward the point where the two roads intersected—and the trucks were about to meet, neither driver letting up off the gas.

Marshall was on the phone to the sheriff when he wasn't hanging on to keep from being bounced all over the cab.

"I suppose you have a plan," Marshall said, sounding a little anxious. "He doesn't look like he's going to give an inch."

Zane didn't answer. His mind was racing. Why start a grass fire? What had been the point?

Suddenly he knew. "Call our brothers," he cried. "Tell them to hightail it to the house. The fire was a diversion!"

The truck was almost to the intersection and so was Zane.

Marshall made the call and then braced himself for

the collision. He must have seen that his brother wasn't slowing down—and neither was the driver of the other pickup.

MRS. CROWLEY ANSWERED the front door on the second knock. She loved to see the expressions of people when they first saw her. Shock, then horror, then a nervous twitch of the eyes as their gazes slid away.

The young woman was even more striking close-up. She couldn't help but think of Clay's last words before his heart attack.

"Don't hurt my daughters." He'd grabbed her arm. "Laura, swear to me you won't hurt my daughters."

Fortunately he'd died before she had to answer.

"Is Emma here?" Dakota asked.

"She's lying down right now, but please come in. She told me to take care of you until she wakes up."

"I don't want to be a bother," Dakota said.

"Don't be silly," Mrs. Crowley said as she stepped aside to let Dakota into the house. "You're no bother. Come on back to the kitchen." She closed the door behind them, surreptitiously locking it. "Emma baked lemon cookies. She insisted you try one with a cup of my tea while you're waiting."

Chapter Thirteen

Hoyt Chisholm stood in the Butte Police Department, shaking inside with both anger and fear. An officer had brought him into a small room and told him to wait, and that he would bring the prisoner in.

Glancing at the chair on the other side of the table, Hoyt was too anxious to sit. He kept reliving that day on Fort Peck Reservoir. Huge waves had rocked the boat as the wind gathered speed and churned up the water from miles down the lake. He'd never seen waves like that and wanted to turn back but Laura had insisted they keep going.

Nor would she wear a life jacket even though she'd told him she couldn't swim. He hadn't wanted the day to turn into one of their horrible fights, so he hadn't made her put the life jacket on. For all these years, he'd regretted that maybe the most.

If she'd been wearing a life jacket, she wouldn't have drowned. Or been able to escape and perpetrate the cruel and inhuman hoax she'd pulled on him.

If she was really alive.

He knew she had to be. Everyone else believed it now, even Sheriff McCall Crawford. Aggie Wells had believed it. Emma, too.

Was the reason he didn't want to believe it because it would mean he'd not only fallen in love with a monster, but he'd married her?

He thought of how he'd nearly drowned diving into the water looking for Laura. Shuddering, he remembered the cold darkness of the water and felt the horror that Laura was down there fighting for her life and he had let her die.

In a body of water as large as Fort Peck, no one had been surprised that her body was never found.

He closed his eyes, hating that he'd married so quickly after her death. By then the adoption had gone through and he had six sons to care for. Tasha had loved them all so and he'd wanted so badly for the boys not to have to grow up without a mother.

Tasha's horseback-riding accident had been ruled just that, an accident. But he knew that if Laura was alive, she'd killed her. Just as she'd killed the next woman who'd come into his life, Krystal.

Laura had tried to frame him for Krystal's murder—just as she was now trying to frame his son. That thought sent a tidal wave of rage roaring through him.

He opened his eyes, fury trumping his terror at coming face-to-face with his dead wife. Whatever Laura's problem, it was with him. She'd taken it out on his wives and now one of his sons. He would stop her. If he had to do it with his bare hands.

He heard footfalls outside the room. The echo grew louder and he braced himself. Was a man ever ready for something like this? The footfalls stopped outside the door. The knob turned, the door swung open and two police officers escorted a dark-haired woman into the room.

She had her head down, but he recognized something familiar in the way she moved. She was the right height, the right body type and even appeared to be close to the age Laura would be now.

One of the police officers motioned for Hoyt to move behind the table.

He stumbled into the chair, gripping the sides as the other officer brought the woman all the way into the room and instructed her to sit down.

She did as she was told.

He watched her slowly lift her head. Her gaze met his.

Hoyt flinched as he looked into the familiar bright blue of her eyes. A sound came out of him, half cry, half curse. *"Laura."*

"I'M SORRY EMMA WASN'T feeling well," Dakota said as she took a seat at the kitchen table. She could see the smoke from the grass fire and silently prayed that Zane and the rest of the firefighters would be safe.

"You don't mind staying with my stepmother?" Zane had said on the way to the ranch.

"Of course not. Emma is delightful."

"She is, isn't she?" he'd said with a laugh. "I have to warn you, though. She'll ply you with cookies or cakes and try to find out everything about the two of us. She'll have us married by the time we get the fire out."

Dakota laughed.

Zane had taken her hand. "Do I need to tell you how crazy I am about you?"

She'd met his gaze and shaken her head. Looking into those blues, she had seen how he felt about her. She was just as crazy about him.

"Well, just in case you don't know, I...I...I'm crazy about you."

She'd laughed, shaking her head. "I love you, too, Zane," she'd said as he pulled up to where the others were battling the fire.

Marshall had come up to Zane's side window then. The next thing she knew she was driving one of the ranch pickups with an empty water tank on the way back down to the house and leaving Zane without another word.

He hadn't said he loved her. She tried not to think about that as she watched the billowing smoke on the horizon, her heart in her throat.

"Do you take milk in your tea?" Mrs. Crowley asked, drawing her attention back to the kitchen.

"No, thank you." Actually, she didn't drink tea, but she wanted to be polite so she said nothing more. One cup of tea wouldn't kill her. She just hoped Zane and the rest of the men were able to get the fire out, and soon.

Something about Mrs. Crowley made her uncomfortable, she thought as she looked over at the housekeeper. The woman had come as a shock. When she'd opened the door, Dakota had been taken aback not so much by the disfigurement, though she hadn't been expecting it, than the look in her one dark eye.

The woman seemed to look through a person.

Dakota shivered at the thought.

"Would you like a sweater?" Mrs. Crowley asked. She had her back to Dakota but she'd seen her shiver?

Dakota realized she'd seen her in the reflection in the microwave door next to her. The woman had been watching her. If Dakota hadn't been creeped out enough by the housekeeper before, she was now.

Mrs. Crowley hurriedly made a cup of tea for Dakota Lansing. She could feel time running out and knew she was cutting this one way too close. Anything could go wrong. She was usually much more organized. Maybe she was losing her touch.

She had planned on ending this quickly—her first day on the Chisholm ranch. Being back in this house had been excruciating. At the time, she hadn't been able to stand even the thought of spending another day here with Emma and Hoyt.

She'd waited until she'd heard Emma coming downstairs that first day. She'd been ready, the coffee made, a cup prepared for Hoyt's fourth wife.

The moment Emma walked in, she'd turned and said, "I have your coffee ready." She'd turned, cup in hand, knowing that Emma took hers black and strong.

"I thought *I* was an early riser," Emma said, clearly unhappy that she didn't have the kitchen to herself.

"I like to get an early start." She was still holding the cup of coffee out, a small tasteless dose of poison carefully stirred into the black brew. Fast and simple sometimes was the best.

"I really don't want you waiting on me," Emma had said as she took the cup. "I appreciate your thoughtfulness, but coffee's been bothering my stomach."

Mrs. Crowley had watched in horror as Emma poured the contents of the cup into the sink. She proceeded to wash out the cup, then pulled down a mug to make herself a cup of tea.

"I can do that," Mrs. Crowley said, trying to keep the frustration from her voice.

"Like I said, I won't have you waiting on me or Hoyt. We like doing for ourselves. I'm sure we explained that you are merely here to help with the housework and some of the cooking, when I need help."

All Mrs. Crowley had been able to do was nod, but she'd been fuming inside.

"I don't want you working too hard," Emma had said.

"I'm capable—"

"I know," her boss said, cutting her off. "But I hope you will be more of a friend than a..."

"Servant?" She could have told the impossible woman that there was more of a chance of that than ever becoming Emma's friend.

"No, more like family," Emma had said, and gave her a smile. "We really want you to feel at home here, Cynthia."

That's when she'd corrected her. "I prefer you call me Mrs. Crowley."

Not that it had stopped Emma from trying to get close to her. Her plan a failure, Mrs. Crowley had become intrigued by the woman and found herself amused enough that she'd felt no need to rush this. She began studying Emma Chisholm, curious about Hoyt's fourth wife.

And all that time, Emma had been curious about her, studying her, spying on her. When she thought about it, the whole thing was actually funny.

But now as she fixed Dakota's tea, she reminded herself that she was finally taking actions that would culminate in the end she had needed for so long.

She would have to hurry, though, and that made her a little sad. But all good things had to come to an end, she told herself as she turned with two cups of tea in her hands. "Emma says I make the best tea she has ever tasted. I hope you like it."

HOYT CHISHOLM WAS GLAD he was sitting down. He stared at Laura, unable to believe his eyes. She'd aged, of course, in the past thirty years. They both had.

But she still looked enough like the woman he'd fallen in love with and married that he would have known her anywhere.

"How did you survive that day in the lake?" he asked. "I dove and dove for you and…"

She stared back at him. "I don't know what you're talking about. My name is Sharon Jones. I've never seen you before in my life."

He looked into her blue eyes. He was still so shocked to see her again that he knew he wasn't thinking clearly. Everyone kept telling him she was alive, but he hadn't believed it until this moment.

"If you don't know who I am, then…" Then she couldn't have been the one who had terrorized him and his family. She couldn't have killed his other wives. She couldn't have framed Zane.

"You're…lying," he said, telling himself this woman was Laura. He felt the weight of what that meant. It brought with it all the ramifications of what this woman had done to him and his family.

What scared him was whether or not the police would be able to prove it. What if they couldn't lock this woman up and throw away the key? He and Emma and his sons would have to live the rest of their lives in fear of what Laura would do next.

"You're a liar and a murderer," he said.

She shook her head slowly and gave him a small half smile. "You're…mistaken."

She even *sounded* like Laura. No one could look this much like his first wife or sound so much like her, unless…

He'd been so shocked to see her that for a moment he'd forgotten what the woman was capable of doing to him. She'd always messed with his mind. Her faked death, her affair with Clay Lansing—she'd put him through hell and had no intentions of stopping.

"She's Laura," he told the cops as he got to his feet. "Get a DNA sample from her and you'll be able to prove this woman is lying. She's wanted for murder in Whitehorse. I'll testify that she is my first wife, Lorraine Baxter Chisholm."

The woman looked up at him as one of the cops helped her to her feet. "You're wrong. Dead wrong."

He shook his head. If she wasn't Laura, then she was her twin sister. "It's her."

As the officer started to take her out of the room, she leaned toward Hoyt and whispered. "Are you really willing to stake your life on it? Or Emma's?"

Her words didn't surprise him. But when she gave him that half smile again, he realized where he'd seen it before—and where the real Laura Chisholm was right now.

DAKOTA TOOK ONE of the lemon cookies as Mrs. Crowley placed a cup of tea in front of her.

"Emma tells me that you recently lost your father," Mrs. Crowley said.

"Yes."

"I'm sorry. I understand he raised stock for rodeos."

Dakota didn't really want to talk about her father. "Yes." She wished Emma would wake up from her nap soon. The housekeeper continued to stare at her with that one dark eye, making her nervous.

She looked toward the kitchen door, hoping to see Emma's friendly face. Instead, she saw something odd.

Part of an apron was sticking out from the under the door of the pantry.

Mrs. Crowley followed her gaze. Dakota couldn't miss the change in the woman's expression.

"Why don't you finish your tea and I'll check on Mrs. Chisholm," the housekeeper said.

Dakota nodded mutely. Emma kept her kitchen spotless. Dakota had noticed when she'd helped her with the desserts the other night. She'd commented then about what a wonderful kitchen it was.

"It's my domain. Everything I wanted in a kitchen. Everything in its place," Emma had said. "I have my sons and husband trained not to touch anything in here. I try my best to keep Mrs. Crowley out as well." She'd made a face. "The woman never puts anything back where it goes. I swear, she'd rearrange everything if I let her."

Mrs. Crowley rose from her chair. Dakota picked up her teacup. She hadn't taken more than a sip. The tea tasted bitter and she didn't want any more of it. She pretended to drink, hoping she could get rid of it when Mrs. Crowley went to check on Emma.

Dakota waited until the woman left the room, then quickly got up and dumped the tea down the drain before hurrying back to the table.

She'd barely sat down again when Mrs. Crowley appeared in the kitchen doorway. Dakota jumped, even more nervous now. She'd come too close to being caught. Why hadn't she just told the woman she didn't like tea?

She hurriedly picked up one of the cookies and took a bite, hoping Mrs. Crowley didn't notice that her hand was shaking as she did.

Mrs. Crowley stood at the end of the kitchen table watching her. "You like her cookies?"

Dakota nodded. "They're delicious. She told me she loves to bake."

"Can't keep her out of the kitchen," Mrs. Crowley said.

Dakota noticed the housekeeper had her hand in the pocket of the apron she wore and she seemed to be standing more upright than she had before.

"You remind me of your father."

Dakota's gaze shot to the woman's face, settling on the one dark eye. "What?"

"Your father. I knew him."

Dakota stared at the woman. "You knew my father?"

"You didn't drink your tea," Mrs. Crowley said.

The swift change of topic threw her for a moment.

"I'm sorry, I thought you just said you knew my father."

"As a matter of fact, we had a very short, intense affair when you were two."

Dakota felt her eyes widen in alarm at the woman's words—and the gun she pulled from her apron pocket. It was a short, snub-nosed revolver and it was pointed right at Dakota's heart.

"You could have made it so much easier if you had only drank your tea like a good girl," Mrs. Crowley said. "I cared about your father. I could have been happy with him had it not been for you. I've never liked children."

"Courtney." The word had slipped out.

"Yes, your sister."

"She's your daughter?" Dakota was still trying to make sense of what she was hearing—and seeing.

"I gave birth to her, if that's what you mean."

"You're…"

Mrs. Crowley smiled. "I used to be Laura Chisholm. Get up. We're going for a ride."

"Where's Emma?"

"Don't worry, she's coming with us."

The gravity of the situation was just starting to sink in. Hoyt was in Butte, his sons were fighting a grass fire and Dakota was looking down the barrel of a gun held by a crazy woman and known killer. She hated to think what this woman had done to Emma, let alone Courtney.

"What are you going to do with us?"

"If it makes you feel any better, before your father died he pleaded with me to promise that I wouldn't hurt you," Laura Chisholm said, then laughed. "Unfortunately he died before I promised him anything."

"You were there when he died." Hadn't she known that was the case? "You and Courtney. You must have taken him to the hospital. Or Courtney—"

"Don't be naive. I gave him something that caused the heart attack, why would I try to save him? Courtney took him, but not until I was sure he wouldn't survive."

Dakota took a step toward the woman, her anger overpowering her common sense. She wanted to take the gun away from this woman and—

"I wouldn't do that," Laura said. "I don't care where

you die but if you ever want to see your sister again, you will do what I tell you."

Dakota watched as Laura popped out the white contact from her eye without ever letting the gun trained on Dakota waver. She popped the other contact out and stared at Dakota with two familiar blue eyes. Courtney had inherited her mother's blue eyes.

EMMA STIRRED, EYELIDS flickering. Her body felt like it was made of lead weights. She didn't think she could move and didn't try for a few moments.

As her eyes finally managed to stay open, she looked around and saw that she was lying on the floor of the pantry.

Had she fallen? Fainted? She tried to sit up and found her muscles so lethargic it took all of her effort.

She was partway up into a sitting position when memory flooded her and she froze, listening.

Voices. She listened, recognizing Mrs. Crowley's monotone. It took her a moment to place the other voice. Dakota Lansing.

Emma sat up the rest of the way, thinking only that she had to save Dakota. She felt her head spin from the sudden movement and thought she might pass out.

She took a moment, trying to clear her head, her thoughts. How did she think she was going to save Dakota when she wasn't even sure she could get to her feet?

As she listened, she felt her blood turn to ice. Mrs. Crowley was Laura Chisholm. The woman had been living in their house all this time? Her heart pounded at the thought of the murderer this close to them.

But hadn't she known something was wrong? Hadn't

she been spying on the woman? She would never have guessed, though, that Mrs. Crowley was Laura Chisholm. Her disguise was too good. Now Emma understood why the woman had kept them all at arm's length. Finally, Emma knew the woman's biggest secret of all.

She heard Mrs. Crowley say, "I guess I don't need to check on Mrs. Chisholm. I hear her getting up now."

She'd heard her moving in the pantry.

From the conversation, Emma knew she didn't have much time. Mrs. Crowley had drugged her, and now the woman had Dakota and was planning on taking them to Courtney.

Emma, even through the haze of whatever she'd been drugged with, was betting the drive would be eleven miles round-trip.

She struggled to her feet. She knew she couldn't fight off the woman she'd known as Mrs. Crowley. All she could do was try to leave a message for Hoyt or the boys when they returned.

She looked around for something to write with and spotted her chalkboard on the back of the pantry door where she made her grocery lists.

Hurriedly, she grabbed a piece of chalk and as quietly as possible, began to write.

Chapter Fourteen

Hoyt called the house immediately, his heart dropping when the phone rang and rang. He left a message for Emma to call him at once.

Then he started to call Sheriff McCall Crawford as he watched the police take the woman he'd thought was Laura back to her cell.

She turned once to look back at him and mouthed, "Too late."

And then she was gone through a door.

Hoyt thought if he had to look at her another minute, he would have gone for her throat.

He'd call the sheriff and his sons on the way to the plane. He needed to get home as quickly as possible. Fortunately, he'd be flying back, but still it would take him too long. That had been the plan, though, hadn't it?

Hoyt couldn't take that thought any further because he knew the rest of her plan. Emma. The thought of losing her was almost his undoing. Ahead he saw the plane and pilot waiting for him.

As he hurried to the plane, he knew this was all his fault. He'd invited the woman into his house. Once as his wife. Now as his housekeeper.

Laura must be ecstatic that she'd fooled him so easily. She'd played him, getting him out of town, far from the ranch and Emma. He prayed he was wrong, but the more the thought about it, he knew Mrs. Crowley was Laura. He racked his brain. Had Laura ever mentioned a twin sister?

He couldn't remember, but the woman he'd just seen at the police station was a close relative, there was no doubt about that. And right now, the woman wasn't going anywhere. The police would be able to hold her until they could get to the bottom of this.

If Laura hurt Emma…

His heart ached from trying to hold in his terror. He had married a monster. Or had he made her that way?

Hoyt didn't know. He just hoped he'd get a chance to ask her—before he killed her.

McCALL HADN'T GOTTEN MUCH sleep last night. The baby had kicked the entire night, it seemed. She'd called in and told the dispatcher she'd be running a little late.

"Can you stay within cell phone range today?" she asked Luke.

"The baby?" His eyes lit when he asked. He smiled as he placed a large hand on her abdomen and felt the baby kick.

She smiled and covered his hand with hers. Her undersheriff Nick Giovanni would be back tomorrow to take over. She was more than ready.

She was hoping for a slow day at the office when her cell phone rang.

Luke shot her a look. "Whatever it is—"

"Sheriff Crawford," she said, taking the call. She listened, avoiding Luke's gaze and trying not to let her true feelings show in her expression. "Don't worry, Hoyt, I'm on my way."

"Hoyt Chisholm? I thought he'd gone to Butte to identify his first wife."

"She wasn't Laura. But he thinks he knows where Laura is." She reached for her shoulder holster.

"I'm going with you."

She started to argue but felt the baby kick. Her stomach cramped and for a moment she held her breath, knowing Luke was watching her intently.

"All right." Even though Luke was a game warden, he'd had the same law enforcement training and was often called in when there was a need.

"Where does he think Laura is?" Luke asked as they headed for her patrol SUV.

"Chisholm ranch. He thinks Laura has been masquerading as his housekeeper, Mrs. Crowley."

Luke let out a low curse. "And Emma?"

"Hoyt tried the house and couldn't raise anyone, but they could all be at that grass fire I heard called in earlier. It's under control, but apparently Emma is missing and so is Mrs. Crowley."

ZANE COULD SEE THE DRIVER of the pickup and knew the man wasn't going to slow down. He was betting that the man driving the truck was the escaped prisoner from California and had nothing to lose and everything to gain if he got away.

"Zane." Marshall sounded worried. "Zane, I quit playing chicken when I was fourteen."

At the speed that they were traveling, the two pickups were going to meet at the same time where the two roads intersected.

"I'm not letting him get away," Zane said, and kept the pedal floored.

He watched the pickup out of the corner of his eye growing closer and closer. He saw Marshall reach for the dash to brace himself for the crash they both knew was coming.

At the last moment, the driver of the other truck veered to the left. Zane hit his brakes and cranked his wheel to the right, but he was still going too fast to keep from hitting the other truck.

The driver's side of Zane's pickup smashed into the passenger side of the other truck, driving it farther up the road and out into the open pasture. As Zane fought to keep control of his pickup, the other driver hit a dry irrigation ditch.

Zane swerved away, tires digging into the dirt, the truck rocking wildly.

"He's losing it," Marshall said as the other truck rolled. It churned up a cloud of dust as it rolled a second time and came to rest on its top out in the middle of the pasture.

When Zane got his pickup stopped at the edge of the road, he and Marshall jumped out and ran toward the truck. The driver had kicked out the windshield and was trying to climb out. The man matched the mug shot the sheriff had provided them of the third escaped prisoner so they could keep an eye out for him.

The escaped felon crawled out, bloody and bruised. He was hurt badly enough that he didn't put up a fight, just lay on his back in the grass.

"I need a doctor," the man cried. "You almost killed me."

"Where is Courtney Baxter?" Zane demanded.

"I'm not saying anything without a lawyer," the man said.

"I'll take care of him," Marshall said, no doubt seeing that his brother wanted to beat the truth out of the man. He grabbed some rope from the back of the pickup and began tying up the escaped prisoner for the ride to the sheriff's department.

Zane's cell rang. "Is everything all right at the house?" he asked when he saw that it was his brother Dawson calling.

"No one's here."

"What?" He looked at Marshall. "He says there's no one there."

"Wait a minute," Dawson said on the other end of the line. "I just found a note from Mrs. Crowley saying that they have gone into town."

Zane was shaking his head. "I'm going to the house," he called to Marshall, who signaled him to go.

Running to his pickup, he leaped in and tore down the road toward the ranch house. Emma wouldn't go into town, not with her stepsons fighting a grass fire burning down the road. She'd be baking something for when they finished with the fire.

He prayed he was wrong about the fire being a diversion. But the timing of the fire was too much of a coincidence. And now Emma, Dakota and Mrs. Crowley were gone?

He could see the house in the distance. Zane raced toward it, his heart in his throat. He kept seeing Dakota's face, remembering their lovemaking.

Why in the hell hadn't he told her that he loved her?

As the house loomed ahead, he prayed Dakota was all right.

"DID SHE HURT YOU?" Dakota asked Emma as they bounced along the road in the ranch pickup. Dakota was driving; Emma sat in the middle with Laura Chisholm holding a gun on her.

"No." Emma had been pretending to doze off and on from the time Dakota had helped Laura put her in the pickup.

"Just keep your eye on the road," Laura snapped. She'd peeled the scar off her face and no longer looked anything like Mrs. Crowley.

"Why are you doing this?" Dakota asked, trying to keep the fear out of her voice. She'd heard all about Laura Chisholm, knew at least some of the horrible things she'd done and suspected there was even worse they didn't know about. Dakota couldn't bear to think of this woman with her father.

"You wouldn't understand," Laura said, and leaned down a little to look into Emma's face. Emma had her eyes closed and her head on Dakota's shoulder.

As they'd been leaving the house, Emma had leaned heavily on her and seemed completely out of it. Until she'd whispered, "Be ready once we reach the well house." Then she had touched her fingers to her lips.

Dakota had nodded and squeezed her hand.

Now she wondered how Emma had known where they were going even before Laura had begun barking out orders.

"Can you drive any slower?" Laura snapped.

Dakota gave the pickup a little more speed. The road was narrow and bumpy as it cut through pasture. As they dropped over a hill, the house disappeared behind them.

"No one is coming to save you," Laura assured her

as she caught Dakota looking in the rearview mirror. "That's a nasty fire that could destroy most of their pasture on that side of the ranch. They aren't going to stop fighting the fire to save you."

Clearly, this woman was behind the fire. She'd managed to get everyone away from the house. Dakota wondered how the housekeeper had started the fire and realized it must have been the third escaped prisoner from California.

"Emma, I'm surprised you don't want to ask about me and Hoyt," Laura taunted.

Emma seemed to stir. "Hoyt?"

Laura laughed. "You do realize that you're not even legally married, since I am alive and well?"

Alive, yes. Well? Dakota thought not. She was just grateful she hadn't drunk the tea the woman had made her. She feared neither she nor Emma would still be alive for this little trip.

As Dakota drove over another hill, she saw the creek through a stand of pines and beyond that, what appeared to be a small stone building with an old waterwheel on one side and a cistern on the other.

AT THE HOUSE, ZANE THREW the pickup into Park and jumped out. As he was running toward the door, he noticed that the truck Mrs. Crowley drove was gone. Someone had left, maybe all three of them, but they hadn't gone to town. Of that he was sure.

He hit the front door, burst through it and into the house, already calling Dakota's name as he ran.

"Dakota!" The house felt empty long before he reached the large kitchen.

He glanced upstairs. "Dakota?" Taking the stairs

two at a time, he charged up to the next floor, all the time telling himself there was no one here. But he had to be sure.

He hadn't passed anyone on the main road but that didn't mean anything. There were numerous back roads on the ranch.

At the bottom of the stairs, he glanced toward the kitchen and noticed two teacups sitting on the table along with a plate of cookies.

Emma would never leave her kitchen without cleaning everything up.

He stepped in and noticed another teacup in the sink. The pantry door was ajar as well.

His phone rang, making him jump. For a moment he thought it was going to be Dakota. He imagined her telling him that she and Emma had gone for a drive with Mrs. Crowley to see the fire.

"Zane?"

It was his brother Marshall. "Is everything all right there?"

"No one's here, just like Dawson said. The pickup Mrs. Crowley has been using is gone."

"Zane, earlier Emma was telling me that she'd been spying on Mrs. Crowley. Apparently the old gal's been going out late at night and not coming back until the wee hours of the morning. She was telling me about it when I saw the fire. She thought Mrs. Crowley might have been meeting a man somewhere on the ranch."

Zane didn't even want to ask why Emma had been spying on the housekeeper. Racing to the far wing, Zane knocked at the housekeeper's door. No answer. He tried the knob. Locked. If he was wrong, his father would not be happy.

He stepped back, lifted his leg and kicked at the door. One more kick and the frame shattered, the lock broke and the door swung in.

The room was immaculate. In fact, it didn't even look as if anyone was staying here.

"Mrs. Crowley?" He stepped in. "Mrs. Crowley?" The bathroom door was ajar. He pushed it all the way open. Empty.

As he turned to leave, he spotted the framed photograph and froze in midstep.

It was a photograph of his father and a woman he'd never seen before. Why would Mrs. Crowley have a photograph of his father and some woman?

He stepped over to the picture and picked up the silver frame. His father looked incredibly young. Behind him was the original ranch house before the later additions, so that meant the woman in the photograph had to have been his father's first wife, Laura.

His gaze went to the woman in the photo. He felt his heart drop to his stomach. The frame slipped from his fingers and hit the floor, the glass shattering.

Laura Chisholm was Mrs. Crowley? She'd been living here all these months, right under their roof?

His cell phone rang. His father. He quickly answered it.

EMMA CONTINUED TO ACT as if she was still suffering from the drug Laura had given her. Through her half-closed eyes, she watched the landscape she had come to love blur past the window of the pickup.

Laura had a small, snub-nosed pistol pressed against her side. Emma felt the cold, hard metal with each bump that the pickup hit as Dakota drove them away from the prairie and up into the foothills.

Out of the corner of her eye, she saw the blackened, scorched earth from the grass fire off to the east. By now her sons would have the flames out and possibly be heading back to the house. She could only hope that they would find the note she'd left in the pantry.

"Don't you want to talk about it?" Laura asked.

Emma raised her head just a little to glance sideways at the woman. She looked so different now without the scarred face, the sightless eye. What gleamed in her two blue eyes was a brittle hatred that made her inwardly flinch.

"I would think you'd have questions for me. Don't you want to know how I survived, how I killed Tasha and Krystal, how I framed your stepson with the help of my daughter?"

Did any of that matter now? Emma didn't think so. "You're sick."

Laura laughed. "I'm no sicker than your friend Aggie."

That reminder stirred something in Emma. She had to tamp it down to keep from showing Laura that she wasn't as drugged as she was pretending.

"I know you killed her," Emma said, slurring her words.

"I hated doing it, though. I admired Aggie. We had a lot in common."

Aggie would have looked beyond Mrs. Crowley's disguise and not been fooled, Emma thought, then remembered that Aggie was dead because Laura had ultimately fooled her somehow as well.

"Why don't you just kill me?" Emma said. "Let Dakota go."

Laura smiled. "I'm afraid I've had to change my plans. You know, if you had drank that first cup of coffee I fixed you the morning after I started my job, it would have been all over right then. No one else would have gotten hurt."

Emma remembered the anger and frustration she'd seen in Mrs. Crowley's expression that morning. She'd misinterpreted it as the woman simply trying to establish herself in the house, the kitchen in particular.

"You could have poisoned me at any time after that," Emma said.

Laura chuckled. "You amused and intrigued me. I liked watching you, knowing that I could kill you at any time—and you had no idea who I was."

"That must have made you very happy." They were close to the old well house now. Emma cut her gaze to Dakota. The young woman was strong and determined, her hands on the wheel sure. Emma knew she could trust Dakota to put up a fight when the time came. She just hoped that she didn't get her killed.

"Park here," Laura ordered. She couldn't help being disappointed. She'd expected more out of Emma. She regretted giving her a drug that, while it had allowed Emma to regain consciousness, made her pathetically docile. She'd hoped for more fight out of her.

"Give me the keys," she told Dakota, who turned off the ignition and handed over the keys.

Laura saw them both looking expectantly toward the old stone well house and stone water tank.

"Let's go see Courtney," Laura said. "I know how

badly you want to see your sister. But remember. If you try anything, I will shoot Emma, then shoot you *and* Courtney."

"You would kill your own daughter?" Dakota demanded.

"I told you. I don't like children. Especially my own."

"What did my father ever see in you?"

Laura laughed. "I was beautiful and sexy and he was broken after your mother's death. I was touched by that kind of anguished love and wished Hoyt loved me half as much."

That got a small rise out of Emma. "Maybe he would have loved you more if you hadn't cheated on him."

Laura opened the pickup door and, keeping the barrel of the gun buried in Emma's side, pulled her out.

"You know nothing about it," she snapped, hating that she'd let Emma get to her. She couldn't have been more jealous of Emma than she was at that moment. Hoyt adored Emma. The two couldn't keep their hands off each other. He'd never been like that with her.

At the door to the well house, she tossed the key to the padlock to Dakota. The stone building had been perfect for her needs. It had no windows, only one door and was almost six miles from the ranch. Nor did anyone ever come up this way.

Laura remembered it because Hoyt had brought her out here the only time she'd ridden a horse with him.

"Open it."

DAKOTA CAUGHT THE KEY. Laura still had the gun pressed into Emma's side, a hand gripping her arm. Emma gave a slight shake of her head. Apparently she didn't want to try to do anything until they got inside.

She inserted the key into the padlock, fearing what they would find inside this odd building. The door was made of metal and had rusted over the years. She had to push hard to get it to open.

As it swung in, Dakota blinked. The only light in the stone structure came from the now open doorway and from four small openings high above in the circular stone walls.

The walls were smooth and there were several old watermarks on them. Dakota realized that this was part of the cistern used for water storage.

She spotted her sister in the shadows and felt a surge of relief. Courtney was alive. For a moment, that was all that mattered. Then she heard the rattle of chains and noticed the handcuff around Courtney's right wrist. The other end of the chain was attached to a pipe that ran along the wall.

Courtney began to cry at the sight of her. "Dakota, how did you—" The rest of her sister's words died on her lips as she saw Laura and Emma come into the room.

"A little family reunion," Laura said.

Courtney seemed to cower, a look of despair on her face. Dakota noticed that she was dressed in a pair of old jeans, a soiled T-shirt and sneakers. There were several containers that looked as if they had contained food stacked in the corner.

"You've kept my sister here chained to a pipe like an animal?" Dakota said, turning on Laura.

"Let's not forget that *your sister* was in on framing your boyfriend," the woman said.

"I haven't forgotten," Dakota said.

"I thought it was just a joke," Courtney cried. "I didn't know...." Her eyes filled with tears again as she bit off the rest of the lie. "Oh, Dakota, I'm so sorry."

As Laura started to shove Emma into the room, Dakota caught her signal. Emma whirled around, taking Laura by surprise, and knocked the gun from her hand. It skittered across the concrete floor. Dakota dove for it.

She heard Emma let out a cry and heard Courtney yell a warning. As her hand closed over the gun she was kicked hard in the side, knocking the air out of her.

Then Laura was on her, slamming her head against the concrete floor. Dakota felt blood run down into her left eye as she tried to fight the woman off. For her age, Laura was surprisingly strong and she fought dirty. She grabbed a handful of Dakota's hair, jerking her head back as she wrenched the gun from her hands.

In an instant, Laura was on her feet and holding the gun on them.

Dakota rolled over, wiping blood from her eye. Emma had gotten to her feet, but Laura had been too fast for her to intervene. She backed up as Laura swung the barrel of the gun toward her.

"Stupid. Stupid. Stupid," Laura said, sounding breathless and yet excited. "I should just shoot you right now. If Dakota moves a muscle, I will."

Dakota froze where she was on the floor as the woman backed her way to the open doorway.

"You aren't going to leave again," Courtney cried. "Please, Mother."

"Don't call me that. You were just a mistake of nature," Laura snapped. "My use for you is over. You wanted to get to know your sister? Well, now's your chance."

"Who is the woman the Butte police have in custody?" Emma asked.

"My cousin. People always thought we were sisters, we're so much alike. She owed me a favor," Laura said with a shrug.

Emma was just thankful that Hoyt was in Butte. By now he would realize he'd been sent on a wild goose chase, but he'd be safe from this woman.

"You know Hoyt will never remarry," Laura said.

"Yes, I know. Is that really all you want, for him to never find happiness with another woman?" Emma asked.

"You make it sound so simple." Laura shook her head. "I *loved* him. I should have been enough, but then suddenly he tells me he's adopting three infant sons and talking about getting another three who needed homes."

"Hoyt loves children," Emma said.

"Yes, but I don't."

"Clearly," Dakota said. "Anyone who could chain up her own daughter and keep her prisoner out here…"

"Don't judge me," Laura snapped, and waved the gun at her.

"You have what you want," Emma said quickly. "Let Courtney and Dakota go. By the time they walk back to the house, I'll be dead and you will be long gone."

Laura smiled. "I thought killing you would be enough, but I was wrong. By the time Hoyt gets back to the ranch, you'll be gone and so will his sons. He will have nothing left. Only then will he finally know how he made me feel."

With that, Laura stepped out through the door, slamming and locking the airtight metal door behind her as she plunged them into semidarkness.

"She's leaving us to die here," Courtney cried.

"No," Emma said as she quickly moved to Dakota and helped her up. "She's not. Are you badly hurt?"

Dakota shook her head as she heard what sounded like the crank of an old metal wheel. "She's not through with us, is she?"

Emma shook her head.

"What?" Courtney cried. "What are you whispering about?"

Before either could answer they heard the water. It cranked and creaked through the ancient pipes for a few moments before it began to fill the chamber where the three of them were now trapped.

Chapter Fifteen

Courtney let out a scream as water began rushing in around her feet. She tried to pull away but she was still hooked to the old pipe that ran along the wall.

"Stay calm," Emma ordered as she and Dakota hurried over to Courtney.

"I think if we both pull on this pipe we might be able to dislodge it," Dakota said. She met Emma's gaze as they both grabbed hold of the rusty pipe. They could feel the water surging through it. Once it broke, the chamber might fill even faster.

But the water was rising quickly and Courtney was manacled close to the floor. She would drown if they couldn't get her free.

"On the count of three," Emma said. "One, two, three!"

Dakota pulled as hard as she could. She heard Emma straining next to her. The pipe gave only a little.

Courtney began to scream. Water was lapping around their ankles now. A leak had sprung in the pipe. A spray of rust-red water showered over the three of them, drenching them to the skin.

"Courtney," Dakota snapped. "You can help. Grab

hold of the chain and pull on the count of three. One, two, three!"

The pipe came lose and the three of them were sent sprawling in the rising water.

"Okay, we can't panic," Emma said as even more water began to flow into the tanklike room. "I left a message. Someone will find it."

But they both knew there was little chance of Hoyt making it back in time. The rest of the Chisholms were fighting the fire. She and Dakota shared a look.

"Zane will come for me," Dakota said, praying it was true. Courtney was crying, pushing at the water with her hands as it rose to their thighs.

"All we have to do is swim when it gets too deep to stand," Emma said. "Once we reach those small windows up there, the water will rush out. We'll be able to breathe."

Dakota looked up at the four slits in the rock, then at Emma. Neither said anything, but Dakota knew the water wouldn't be able to rush out fast enough to save them, because the slits were too close to the top of the tank.

Their only hope was being found before they drowned.

LUKE HAD INSISTED on driving. "You'll be more comfortable in the passenger seat," he'd said, and McCall knew he'd been watching her. Nor was she feeling well enough to argue the point. She tried to get comfortable, but it was impossible with the baby being so active.

Time was of the essence if Hoyt was right and his housekeeper was Laura Chisholm. As far as Hoyt had known, the two were alone in the house, she told Luke.

"Hasn't this woman been working for them for several months?" Luke asked as he drove toward Whitehorse. She and Luke lived south of town on Luke's folks' old place. He'd built them a beautiful home, which he'd made her wedding present.

"So why would Emma have something to fear now, is that what you're asking?" McCall said. She'd been thinking the same thing. "I wonder if it doesn't have something to do with Zane." She had told him about Courtney Hughes aka Courtney Baxter. "Laura's her mother."

Luke shook his head. "If this Mrs. Crowley is Laura Chisholm, then where is Courtney?"

That was the question, and had been since she'd disappeared the night after her "date" with Zane. He was out on bail and if Courtney didn't turn up, or worse, turned up dead...

"Have you thought any more about what you want to do after the baby is born?" Luke asked.

McCall had her hand on her abdomen. She loved the feel of their child inside her. Safe. But once the baby was born... She flinched as she felt not a cramp, but what could only be a contraction.

"Honey?" Luke said, glancing over at her. "McCall?" He sounded alarmed.

"It's nothing. Just a twinge." That was all it had been, right? The baby moving so much must have caused it.

Suddenly she was scared. She would have gladly faced killers every day than to think about being the mother to this baby.

"Talk to me, McCall. I know something's going on with you."

"It was just a twinge," she said, hoping it was true.

She needed to carry this baby to term. It was a month too early.

"I'm talking about right now. I'm talking about the last eight months," Luke said. "I know you're worried about the baby because we lost the first one, but—"

"I'm scared." The words were out before she could call them back. She hated to admit to Luke how she was feeling. "I'm not sure what kind of mother I'll be. Look at my mother. Ruby was…well, Ruby."

"That's ridiculous," Luke said. "Is that all that's been bothering you? You're nothing like Ruby, thank heaven." He looked over at her and said, "McCall?"

She had another contraction, this one much stronger than the first one. "I think I'm in labor. It just came on so suddenly." She remembered losing the other baby. It had started much like this.

"I'm taking you to the hospital."

She nodded as she heard Luke on the patrol SUV radio calling the sheriff's office. "Halley Robinson is the closest to the Chisholm place. Have them send her," McCall said.

Luke passed on the message as he raced toward the hospital.

McCall prayed her baby would be all right. She was almost to term. But what would she do once the baby was born? She was terrified she might become like her mother.

AFTER THE CALL FROM HIS father, Zane raced back downstairs to the kitchen. Hoyt had already figured out somehow that Mrs. Crowley was Laura.

"You have to stop her," his father had pleaded. "Whatever you have to do."

Zane knew what he was saying. But first he had to find them. If Emma was right and Mrs. Crowley had been going somewhere on the ranch at night...

In the kitchen he noticed the partially opened pantry door—and the hem of Emma's apron sticking out. He quickly moved to it, heart in his throat as he prayed he wouldn't find her—

The pantry was empty. He breathed a sigh of relief, then saw the note on the chalkboard.

Well house. Laura/Crowley. Hurry.

The well house was an old cistern system that hadn't been used in years. Water had been diverted from the creek for storage for low precipitation years back when the ranch was started.

Zane placed a call to his brothers as he ran to his pickup. He told them everything, including what his father had said as he drove toward the well house. "Marshall has taken the third prisoner escapee into jail."

"We have a section of fire we're fighting near the house," Dawson said.

"I can handle this. I just needed you to know. Dad is flying in. He's going to be heading straight for the ranch the minute his plane touches down."

"Find them," Dawson said.

"I will." Zane snapped the phone shut and drove as fast as he could up the road toward the foothills.

LAURA COULD SEE DUST in the distance. She'd told Rex to pick off one after another of the Chisholm brothers.

Now she had a bad feeling he hadn't done as he was told. She should have killed him instead of his mouthy cellmate Lloyd. Lloyd would have gotten the job done.

As she started to climb into the ranch pickup, she

saw the flat tire. For a moment she just stood looking at it.

A flat? It seemed inconceivable that something so ordinary could foil her plans. For years she'd gotten away with murder, literally, because she'd planned every detail meticulously.

Laura glanced toward the road down in the valley again. Dust boiled up behind a rig headed this way fast.

She looked around for a place to hide, telling herself fate was playing right into her hand. She needed a vehicle and someone was bringing her one.

All she had to do was pull the trigger when the time came and then get out of here.

She could hear the water filling the tank and imagined the three women inside panicking. Especially Courtney.

For just an instant, Laura felt badly that Clay Lansing's daughters were part of the collateral damage.

But there was no way Laura could leave the girls alive. Courtney especially was like a loose thread. One little tug and everything would come unraveled.

As the vehicle coming up the road grew near, Laura looked around for a good spot to hide in wait to ambush whoever it was. She needed their vehicle and, one way or another, she planned to get it.

THEY WOULD HAVE TO SWIM soon. The water was rising faster now. Emma realized Laura must have closed off the main cistern tank. With the floodgates open, this tank was filling fast.

Creek water lapped at her waist. The three of them had moved to the edge of the tank closest to the door. They had tried to break down the door but to no avail.

Now they were just saving their energy for when they would have to swim.

"I'm so sorry," Courtney said, not for the first time. "When she contacted me I was just so glad to finally meet my birth mother."

"It doesn't matter now," Dakota said.

"We're going to die, aren't we?"

"No, we're not," Emma snapped. She wished Dakota's sister had her strength and courage. The young woman seemed to have been pampered much of her life. A little hardship and struggle seemed to hone a person for times like this. Courtney hadn't been tested and now, facing the biggest test of her life, was ill prepared.

"Do you hear something?" Courtney asked suddenly.

Over the sound of the water filling the tank, Emma listened. A vehicle.

Courtney brightened. "Someone is coming to save us, just like you said." She was all smiles now.

Emma shared a look with Dakota, who seemed to share her own worry. She hadn't heard Laura leave and now feared that whoever was coming was about to walk right into a trap.

ZANE SLOWED AS HE SAW the ranch pickup parked next to the well house. He'd pulled his shotgun down from the rack behind the pickup seat and had it and his pistol within reach.

Slowly, he pulled up behind the pickup and saw the flat tire. He killed the engine, listening through his open side window.

Where were they? More to the point, where was Laura Chisholm?

That's when he heard the water sloshing around in the old cistern tank. What the hell?

And in that instant, he knew. Jumping out of the truck, he ran to the door.

"Dakota? Emma?" he yelled. He could hear water running in from the creek and the faint sound of voices on the other side.

He tried the door, but it opened inward so the water in the tank would make it impossible to open.

There was only one option. He had to close the head-gates on the creek, divert the water back into the creek and drain the tank as quickly as possible.

He rushed around the side to the headgates. Someone had jammed a crowbar into them, locking the gates open. He was struggling to free the crowbar when he heard the first shot.

A bullet whizzed past his ear. The second shot splintered the wood next to him.

Diving for cover, he used the momentum and his weight to dislodge the crowbar. But the gate was still open, water still filling the tank, just not as quickly.

He peered out, trying to assess where the shots had come from. He didn't need to ask who had just tried to kill him.

Another bullet whizzed past. Laura had to be in the trees up on the side of the hill. He could still hear the water flowing into the tank. In order to drain the tank, he had to get from where he was across twenty yards without cover.

She'd fired three shots, but he didn't doubt she'd come with plenty of ammunition. Nor could he wait her out. The flow into the cistern had slowed almost to a trickle but he had to drain the tank. He didn't know how long Dakota and Emma could stay afloat in there. If they were even still alive.

The thought forced him to move. He pulled out his pistol and hoped he was right about Laura being in the trees on the hillside. It was a chance he had to take. Once he got the drain opened...

He got ready, then, firing as he ran, sprinted toward the cistern. If he could reach it and get on the far side...

DEPUTY HALLEY ROBINSON SAW the smoke and the men putting out the last of the grass fire as she raced down the road toward the Chisholm house.

She recognized her fiancé, Colton Chisholm, on the fire line but she didn't stop. Her orders were to get to the house as quickly as possible and arrest the woman she knew only as Mrs. Crowley.

Halley had to ask the dispatcher to repeat what she'd said.

"The housekeeper is believed to be Laura Chisholm."

Halley still couldn't believe it. She'd seen the cantankerous Mrs. Crowley on numerous occasions when she'd been out to the ranch house. Everyone gave her a wide berth. Halley wasn't sure she'd ever looked the woman in the eye or really studied her face.

Now, as she neared the house, her only thought was of Emma. She'd fallen in love with Colton's stepmother, everyone had. If this report was right, then Laura Chisholm was a killer hell-bent on killing Hoyt's fourth wife—as she had his other two.

Halley parked in front of the house, noticing that the pickup Mrs. Crowley drove wasn't anywhere around. But there was a ranch pickup out front.

Climbing out, she unsnapped her holster, her hand

on the butt of her weapon as she mounted the stairs, crossed the porch and knocked at the door. No answer.

She tried the knob. "Hello?" No answer again.

She made her way to the kitchen, Emma's domain. The house had an eerie feel to it that she didn't like. The moment she saw the cluttered kitchen she knew something was wrong.

Then she saw the note. Mrs. Crowley had written that they had gone into town. But that was marked out and below it was scrawled "Well house, Laura has Emma and Dakota." It was signed "Zane."

Fortunately Colton had taken Halley up to the old well house once on a horseback ride. She ran for her cruiser, called in her ETA and a request for backup she knew wouldn't be coming in time as she raced up the road toward the foothills.

McCALL GLANCED AT THE CLOCK on the wall and felt another hard contraction coming. "Check and see if there has been any word from Halley," she said, her voice strained.

She was worried. There'd been no word on what was going on out at the Chisholm ranch. More and more, she suspected that Hoyt had been right. The house-keeper *was* Laura Chisholm, and everyone knew what that woman was capable of.

"I checked a few minutes ago," Luke said. "Honey, there is nothing you can do but have this baby. Halley can handle herself. So can the Chisholm men."

McCall nodded and tried to breathe through the contraction. Luke was right. There was nothing she could do for Emma or anyone else. She was about to have their baby. She tried to concentrate on breathing.

Just think about your baby.

"Did you call my grandmother?" she asked as the contraction ended.

Luke laughed. "Of course. She'd made it clear she was to be notified the moment you went into labor, and I'm not about to cross Pepper Winchester. Or your mother. Ruby and Red are on their way. Hunt's driving your grandmother in from the ranch."

She smiled and looked into her husband's handsome face. She could feel their baby inside her, ready to come out into the world and make them a family. *This is your world, right here in this room,* she thought.

Another contraction hit. Dr. Carrey stuck his head in the door. He was wearing his Stetson but he'd changed into scrubs.

"Pepper called to tell me not to deliver the baby until she got here, but I've got a rodeo tonight so let's get this baby born," Doc joked as he took off his hat.

McCall saw Luke step outside the room to take a call. She caught his expression before the door closed and realized he was as worried as she was about what was happening at the Chisholm ranch.

"What?" she asked when he came back in.

"Halley, she called in. She's all right."

"And Laura?" McCall asked, her voice breaking as another contraction gripped her.

He shook his head. "They'll get her."

Chapter Sixteen

Zane sprinted toward the cistern, firing the pistol toward the trees as he ran. The air filled with the reports of shots, his and Laura's. He still couldn't tell where she was firing from and right now it didn't matter. As long as he reached the drain and could get it open...

He was ready to dive over the side of the hill to open the drain at the base of the cistern, when he felt the searing heat of a bullet. His left leg collapsed under him and he rolled, still firing. Fortunately, his momentum took him over the edge of the hill.

Rolling down the slope, he came to a stop at the bottom of the well house next to the drain. He knew he was hit; his leg felt on fire, but he was able to crawl over to the drain valve.

He didn't have much time. In order to open the drain he would have to use both hands. And even then he feared it wouldn't be enough. The valve wouldn't have been opened in years. His fear was that he wouldn't be strong enough without some sort of tool.

Blood soaked into the thigh of his jeans. He quickly laid down his pistol and grabbed the valve handle with both hands. It didn't budge. With a curse, he pulled himself up and put all his weight into it. The handle turned a few inches.

He heard the sound of footfalls on loose gravel. Laura was coming. Any moment, she would be down the hill and around the cistern.

Zane put everything he had into turning the handle.

LAURA KNEW SHE'D HIT HIM. She'd seen him go down. He'd been heading to the backside of the cistern where the drain was located. He'd managed to stop the flow of water into the tank. She couldn't hear the women. They would have to be swimming by now. The creek water was cold. They couldn't last long.

By now Courtney would have drowned. That thought gave her a moment's pause as she came off the hillside. Two to go—if she could stop Zane.

Laura smiled to herself. This would be over soon. She had just reached the road when she saw the dust and heard the roar of a vehicle engine. Company. Even from this distance she could make out a sheriff's department patrol SUV. McCall.

"Make my day," she said under her breath. This day was just getting better.

She could hear Zane trying to open the old drain. *Good luck with that,* she thought as the patrol car zoomed up the road. Laura crouched down in front of her pickup to wait. There was time. Even if Zane got the drain open, it would take a while for the water to drain enough to get the door open.

THE HANDLE TURNED. Zane heard a *clunk,* the sound of the lock released. He fell back, pulling the drain lid open. Water began to gush out. Inside the cistern, he heard the faint sound of women's voices. He couldn't make out the words but there were at least two women in there, still alive.

The water was rushing out quickly. If they could just stay afloat a little longer…

Picking up his gun, he knew he couldn't stay here. He would be a sitting duck. Actually, he was surprised Laura hadn't already found him. She would know where he'd been headed. So where was she?

He listened. That's when he heard the sound of a vehicle coming. But there was another noise as well. He looked up and saw a small plane headed in this direction.

DEPUTY HALLEY ROBINSON SLOWED as the well house came into view. Two pickups. The one Mrs. Crowley had been driving. The other must be Zane's.

She didn't see anyone as she pulled up behind Zane's truck. She cut her engine and opened the door, pulling her weapon as she did. Staying behind the driver's side door, she peered around the edge. She could hear water running.

"Zane!" she called. "Zane?"

He appeared at the lower edge of the cistern. She could see that his left leg was soaked with blood. He leaned against the stone structure, a gun in his hand, and motioned for her to stay back.

"Mrs. Crowley is Laura. She's got a gun!" he called.

Halley took in what she could see of the area. No sign of the housekeeper. Or anyone else.

She listened and heard running water. Closer, crickets chirped in the tall grass. The sun beat down. Nothing moved.

Halley never heard her. At the last minute, she sensed the woman behind her. She felt the hair rise on the back of her neck. As she started to swing around, she felt a viselike arm come around her neck. The barrel of a gun jabbed into her back. Her own weapon was wrenched out of her hand.

In the SUV's side mirror, Halley caught a glimpse of the woman she'd known as Mrs. Crowley. The scar was gone. So was the one white eye, the one dark eye. Two very blue eyes burned too brightly from a face that was surprisingly attractive.

She'd always wondered about the first Mrs. Chisholm and what it would be like coming face-to-face with a monster. Now she knew.

"Don't think for a moment that I won't kill you," Laura said.

Halley didn't. She'd almost been killed by someone much tamer than this woman when she worked on the West Coast.

"Zane!" Laura called. "I have Halley." She jabbed the deputy hard in the back.

Halley let out a cry.

Zane appeared at the bottom edge of the cistern again.

"I need you to throw down your gun," Laura said. "Then I need you to toss me your truck keys. If you don't, I will kill your future sister-in-law."

Zane hesitated only a moment. He tossed his gun away from him, then reached into his pocket and pulled out his keys. He threw them up on the road just a few yards from them.

Halley heard the airplane. It sounded as if it was going to land on them as it zoomed just over their heads.

"Today is your lucky day," Laura said, and gave Halley a shove that sent her over the edge of the road and rolling down the slope to the creek.

A moment later, Halley heard a pickup engine fire. Gravel pelted the patrol SUV as Laura spun the tires on the truck and took off down the road.

DAKOTA HEARD THE SOUND of someone trying to open the door. The water had drained down until they could stand, but the cold creek water still pooled around their ankles. They were weak from the exertion of swimming. The cold water had zapped all their strength and all three of them were shivering convulsively. She worried that if they didn't get out soon, they would die of hypothermia.

When the door swung open, the first thing Dakota saw was Zane's face in the bright sunlight that poured in.

She stumbled to him, only then seeing the bandana tied around his thigh, the blood-soaked jeans and the lack of color in his handsome face. He grabbed her, holding her tightly against him as Halley wrapped a blanket around Emma and Courtney and helped them out into the sunshine.

Dakota began to cry as she pulled back to look into Zane's face. She'd feared that she would die in the cistern and never get to see him again. She'd known he'd come for her, prayed that he would be safe.

"We have to get Zane to the hospital," Halley was saying. "He's lost a lot of blood."

As Courtney and Emma climbed into the patrol SUV, Halley helped Dakota get Zane into the back.

Halley gave her a blanket from the back and Zane held her. She couldn't stop shaking.

Halley slid in behind the wheel and took off toward Whitehorse.

"Laura?" Emma asked, her teeth chattering.

"She got away," Halley said.

"I don't think so," Zane said as he motioned out the side window. In the distance they could see the pickup barreling down the road, a cloud of dust boiling up as it went.

A small airplane was coming from the other direction. It was headed right for the pickup.

LAURA SAW THE PLANE COMING directly at her. Hoyt. So this was how it would end, she thought, and sped up. She just hoped she got a good look at his face before she died—and he got a good look at hers.

As the plane roared toward her, sun glinted off its windshield. She squinted, trying desperately to see the man behind the controls as she braced herself for impact.

She'd been so sure he would kill himself before he'd let her get away that she hadn't been paying attention to the road ahead.

At the last minute, the pilot pulled up. The plane's belly practically scraped the top of the pickup's cab—he'd called it that close. It happened so fast. All she could see was the plane out the pickup windshield, then it was gone and she was staring not at the road ahead but open, rugged country.

The road had turned and she hadn't even noticed. She hit the brakes but the pickup was going too fast. It began to skid and hit the edge of the road hard, slamming her against the door.

She fought to get control as the truck dropped down into the ditch. She could see the embankment coming up and braced herself as the pickup went airborne.

The truck plummeted over the embankment and nose-dived into the ground at the bottom. Her head snapped back hard. She saw stars, then darkness before the pickup came to a stop half-buried in dirt and sagebrush not two miles from the Chisholm ranch house she'd once called home.

When she opened her eyes, Hoyt was beside the pickup, staring at her through what was left of the shattered side window. He had a gun in his hand.

"You can't kill me," she said, sneering at him.

He raised the gun as she fumbled for her own weapon. Hadn't she always known this was the way it had to end?

She pulled out her gun, but never got to aim before he fired.

"WOULD YOU LIKE TO SEE your daughter?" The nurse brought the blanket-wrapped bundle over to her and put the infant into her arms.

McCall stared down at her daughter and felt tears rush to her eyes. "She's beautiful."

"Just like her mother," Luke said as he leaned over to look at his daughter.

All McCall could do was stare at the infant in awe. "We did this?"

Luke laughed. "Yes, honey, we did."

"I wondered how I would feel when I held my baby." She looked up at her husband. "There are no words."

"You're going to be a great mother. You know that now, don't you?"

McCall nodded, too choked up to speak. She didn't know if she would be great, but she did know she would give it everything she had. And, unlike her mother, she had Luke.

"They said I have a great-granddaughter," Pepper Winchester said as she stuck her head in the doorway.

McCall smiled at her grandmother and turned the bundle in her arms so Pepper could see her. Pepper's eyes filled at the sight of the infant. She reached for McCall's hand and squeezed it.

McCall fought her own tears at the sight of the grandmother she'd never known until recently crying over this new life. *Strange the twists and turns life takes,* she thought. Her daughter would know her great-grandmother. She would have more family than McCall would ever have been able to imagine. Dozens of cousins, loads of people who loved her.

As if on cue, her own mother came into the room. Ruby stopped a few feet away and seemed to be waiting for an invitation.

"Well, don't just stand there," Pepper snapped at the daughter-in-law she'd denied for twenty-seven years. "Come see your grandbaby."

Ruby smiled and came over to the bed. Her eyes widened. "It's a girl?"

McCall nodded.

"Have you chosen a name?" Pepper asked.

"Tracey, after my father," McCall said, and heard Pepper let out a sob. "Tracey Winchester Crawford." Pepper covered her mouth with her hand for a moment, tears spilling from her eyes, as if fighting to keep from bawling.

Her husband and the man Pepper had loved since she was sixteen came up behind her and put an arm around her. She turned to press her face into his broad chest. Hunt smiled at McCall over his wife's shoulder and mouthed, "Thank you."

"Is that all right with you?" McCall asked her mother.

Ruby nodded. "I know your father would have liked that."

Epilogue

Zane woke in the hospital room to find Dakota asleep in the chair next to his bed and Dr. Carrey standing nearby, writing something in his chart.

"She refused to leave here," Doc said of Dakota, keeping his voice down. "I got her into the only dry clothes we had."

Dakota was dressed in hospital scrubs. She couldn't have looked cuter.

"The bullet didn't hit any bone so I think it should heal nicely," Doc was saying. "You just won't be running any footraces for a while."

"Are Emma and Courtney all right?" he asked. He'd been surprised to see Courtney come out of the cistern, surprised and thankful. All charges against him would be dropped now.

"They're fine. Both were treated and released. You do have another visitor, though. He's been waiting for you to wake up."

Doc left. A moment later, Hoyt came in. He glanced at the sleeping Dakota and smiled. "How are you, son?"

"Doc says I'm going to be fine. Emma and Courtney are all right, too, he said."

His father nodded.

"Did Laura…"

"She's dead."

Zane studied his father's face. "I'm sorry."

Hoyt let out a sound like a cross between a laugh and a sob. "I'm not. I'm just sorry she put my family through so much."

"We're Chisholms. We're pretty resilient."

His father smiled. "Yes," he said. "We are. Well, I best get home. Emma's got the rest of the family building on to the dining room. She says the current one isn't going to be able to hold all of us." He glanced toward Dakota, who was starting to stir. "I suppose she's right about that."

DAKOTA OPENED HER EYES to see Zane grinning at her. She was reminded of the boy she'd known, that cocky rodeo cowboy who used to grin at her just like that.

"Hey, beautiful," he said as he reached for her hand.

She took it and let him pull her out of the chair and into his arms. "Easy, you're injured."

"Doc was just here. I'm fine and as soon as I get out of here…" His grin widened.

She shook her head, wanting to pinch herself. Hadn't this been her girlhood dream? She thought about the diary Courtney had taken, no longer caring if it came to light. She'd been afraid of her feelings for Zane, afraid that he could never feel the way she did for him.

Wasn't that what had made Laura so crazy? She'd believed that her love was greater than Hoyt's and it had driven her insane. If she wasn't half-crazy before that.

"There's something I need to ask you," Zane said, suddenly serious. "This isn't the way I planned it. All the way, racing up to the well house, I had this romantic plan how I was going to ask you to marry me." He shook his head. "But when I woke up to find you asleep in that chair next to my bed…"

"Your sanity came back?" she joked.

His gaze locked with hers. "I realized anywhere is the perfect place and I can't wait another moment. Dakota, marry me. I know this might feel sudden, but we've known each other since we were kids and—"

"Yes," she said, leaning down to kiss him.

He laughed and pulled her down for another kiss.

"Easy, cowboy."

"I love you, Dakota. I've always loved you from the first time I saw you try to ride a sheep. You must have been five at the time. I'd never seen a little girl with so much grit." He laughed. "I was so impressed when that sheep stopped and you did a face-plant in the dirt, and got up and didn't even cry as you dusted yourself off and walked away."

"I went behind the rodeo stands and cried. Mostly I was mad at myself for not staying on longer." She touched his cheek. "I've always loved you. As a matter of fact, I kept a diary and in it I said that someday I was going to marry you."

"And now you are," he said, and started to kiss her again but was interrupted by a sound at the door.

They both turned to find Courtney standing there.

"I'm sorry to interrupt, but I wanted to say goodbye and how sorry I am for everything," her sister said.

"Where are you going?" Dakota asked.

"Back to Great Falls. My mother…" Her voice broke. "My *real* mother, Camilla, wants me to come stay with her awhile until I figure out what I want to do with my life."

"I'm going to walk Courtney out," Dakota said. Zane squeezed her hand.

"Again, I'm sorry, Zane."

He nodded. "Put it behind you, Courtney. We have."

Dakota walked her out. "How are you getting home?"

"I'm taking the bus." Courtney looked away. "Do you think things like this happen for a reason? I mean, that they can completely change your life?"

"I do."

Her sister raised her gaze. "Sometime, I'd like to know more about my father."

Dakota nodded. "We're sisters, Courtney. The same blood runs through our veins. When you're ready, come back. I've always wanted a sister." She stepped up to Courtney and hugged her. Her sister hugged her tight. "Be happy."

"You, too," Courtney said. "You and Zane belong together. Send me a wedding invitation," she said with a grin.

"I won't need to. You're going to be standing right next to me as my maid of honor."

EMMA LOOKED AROUND the large dining room table. *Glad I talked Hoyt into adding on,* she thought with a smile as she took in her family.

A little more than a year ago, she'd come here as a new bride to find she had six rambunctious and wild step-sons all in need of a woman to tame them. To think she'd thought she was the one to find them the perfect mates.

"What are you smiling about?" her father asked. Alonso had finally decided he'd better fly up from California and see how his daughter was doing.

"It's a long story," Emma said as she reached over and took his hand. "Isn't this all wonderful?"

He laughed softly. "God has blessed you."

"Yes." She couldn't have agreed more as she met her

husband's gaze at the opposite end of the table. She took in Halley and Colton, Billie Rae and Tanner, Jinx and Dawson, Alexa and Marshall, Blythe and Logan, and finally Dakota and Zane.

In the past year she'd come close to losing all of them. But the Chisholms had prevailed. They were a strong, determined bunch, just like those who had settled this part of Montana before them. They'd weathered rough storms and yet here they all were, laughing and talking all at once around this table.

Once they got through all the upcoming weddings, there would be grandchildren before long. Hoyt was already talking about getting some small saddles and gentle horses for them. She'd never seen her husband more happy. He'd faced his worst fear, and now here he was among the people who loved him.

Her eyes filled with tears and she had to hastily wipe them as Hoyt rose, tapped his glass to get everyone's attention and said, "I'd like to make a toast."

The room fell silent, all eyes on her handsome, wonderful husband.

"To my family," he said, his voice breaking with emotion. "The Chisholms and the future Chisholms. Long may they live on this ranch and prosper."

"And multiply," Colton said with a grin as he looked over at his wife. Halley blushed.

"Hear, hear," Emma said, and felt tears rush into her eyes. She couldn't wait to be a grandmother, and apparently she didn't have long to wait.

* * * * *

REQUEST YOUR FREE BOOKS!
2 FREE NOVELS PLUS 2 FREE GIFTS!

Harlequin®

INTRIGUE®

BREATHTAKING ROMANTIC SUSPENSE

YES! Please send me 2 FREE Harlequin Intrigue® novels and my 2 FREE gifts (gifts are worth about $10). After receiving them, if I don't wish to receive any more books, I can return the shipping statement marked "cancel." If I don't cancel, I will receive 6 brand-new novels every month and be billed just $4.49 per book in the U.S. or $5.24 per book in Canada. That's a saving of at least 14% off the cover price! It's quite a bargain! Shipping and handling is just 50¢ per book in the U.S. and 75¢ per book in Canada.* I understand that accepting the 2 free books and gifts places me under no obligation to buy anything. I can always return a shipment and cancel at any time. Even if I never buy another book, the two free books and gifts are mine to keep forever.

182/382 HDN FEQ2

Name _____ (PLEASE PRINT) _____

Address _____ Apt. # _____

City _____ State/Prov. _____ Zip/Postal Code _____

Signature (if under 18, a parent or guardian must sign)

Mail to the **Reader Service:**
IN U.S.A.: P.O. Box 1867, Buffalo, NY 14240-1867
IN CANADA: P.O. Box 609, Fort Erie, Ontario L2A 5X3

Not valid for current subscribers to Harlequin Intrigue books.

**Are you a subscriber to Harlequin Intrigue books
and want to receive the larger-print edition?
Call 1-800-873-8635 or visit www.ReaderService.com.**

* Terms and prices subject to change without notice. Prices do not include applicable taxes. Sales tax applicable in N.Y. Canadian residents will be charged applicable taxes. Offer not valid in Quebec. This offer is limited to one order per household. All orders subject to credit approval. Credit or debit balances in a customer's account(s) may be offset by any other outstanding balance owed by or to the customer. Please allow 4 to 6 weeks for delivery. Offer available while quantities last.

Your Privacy—The Reader Service is committed to protecting your privacy. Our Privacy Policy is available online at www.ReaderService.com or upon request from the Reader Service.

We make a portion of our mailing list available to reputable third parties that offer products we believe may interest you. If you prefer that we not exchange your name with third parties, or if you wish to clarify or modify your communication preferences, please visit us at www.ReaderService.com/consumerchoice or write to us at Reader Service Preference Service, P.O. Box 9062, Buffalo, NY 14269. Include your complete name and address.

HI11B

Under Montana's big sky, two lovers will find their way back to one another…if an unsolved murder doesn't pull them apart forever.

A new tale of love, forgiveness and healing from *USA TODAY* bestselling author

B.J. DANIELS

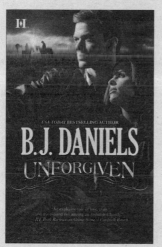

In Beartooth, Montana, land and family is everything. So when Destry Grant's brother is accused of killing Rylan West's sister, high school sweethearts Destry and Rylan leave their relationship behind in order to help their families recover from tragedy.

Years later, Destry is dedicated to her ranch and making plans for the future. Plans that just might include reuniting with the love of her life…until her brother returns to clear his name and the secrets of the past threaten her one chance at happiness.

Coming soon!

*Harlequin Intrigue® presents a new installment
in* USA TODAY *bestselling author
Delores Fossen's miniseries*
THE LAWMEN OF SILVER CREEK RANCH.

Enjoy a sneak peek at KADE.

Kade saw it then. The clear bassinet on rollers, the kind
they used in the hospital nursery.

He walked closer and looked inside. There was a baby,
and it was likely a girl, since there was a pink blanket snuggled around her. There was also a little pink stretchy cap on
her head. She was asleep, but her mouth was puckered as if
sucking a bottle.

"What does the baby have to do with this?" Kade asked.

"Everything. Two days ago someone abandoned her in the
E.R. waiting room," the doctor explained. "The person left
her in an infant carrier next to one of the chairs. We don't
know who did that, because we don't have security cameras."

Kade was finally able to release the breath he'd been
holding. So this was job related. They'd called him in because he was an FBI agent.

But he immediately rethought that.

"An abandoned baby isn't a federal case," Kade clarified,
though Grayson already knew that. Kade reached down and
brushed his index finger over a tiny dark curl that peeked
out from beneath the cap. "You think she was kidnapped or
something?"

When neither the doctor nor Grayson answered, Kade
looked back at them. The anger began to boil through him.
"Did someone hurt her?"

"No," the doctor quickly answered. "There wasn't a
scratch on her. She's perfectly healthy as far as I can tell."

The anger went as quickly as it had come. Kade had handled the worst of cases, but the one thing he couldn't stomach was anyone harming a child.

"I called Grayson as soon as she was found," the doctor went on. "There were no Amber Alerts, no reports of missing newborns. There wasn't a note in her carrier, only a bottle that had no prints, no fibers or anything else to distinguish it."

Kade lifted his hands palms up. "That's a lot of no's. What do you know about her?" Because he was sure this was leading somewhere.

Dr. Mickelson glanced at the baby. "We know she's about three or four days old, which means she was abandoned either the day she was born or shortly after. She's slightly underweight, barely five pounds, but there was no hospital bracelet. We had no other way to identify her, so we ran a DNA test." His explanation stopped cold, and his attention came back to Kade.

So did Grayson's. "Kade, she's yours."

How does Kade react when he finds out the baby is his?

Find out in KADE.
Available this July wherever books are sold.

This summer, celebrate everything Western
with Harlequin® Books!

www.Harlequin.com/Western

INTRIGUE®

USA TODAY BESTSELLING AUTHOR

B.J. Daniels

BRINGS READERS
HER HIGHLY ANTICIPATED SEQUEL

JUSTICE AT CARDWELL RANCH

Six years ago Dana Cardwell found her mother's will in
a cookbook and became sole owner of the Cardwell Ranch
in Big Sky, Montana. Now, happily married and with twins on
the way, Dana is surprised when her siblings, Stacy and Jordan,
show up on the ranch...and trouble isn't too far behind them.
As danger draws closer to the ranch, deputy marshal
Liza Turner quickly realizes that Jordan Cardwell isn't the man
the town made him out to be.

*Catch the thrill October 2 with Harlequin Intrigue®
wherever books are sold!*